# The Lost Sword
# of the
# Confederate Ghost

## *A Mystery in Two Centuries*

by

**Emily C. Monte**

$\overline{\underset{\text{KIDS}}{\underset{}{\text{M}}}}^{\text{TM}}$ WHITE MANE KIDS

This White Mane Books publication
was printed by
Beidel Printing House, Inc.
63 West Burd Street
Shippensburg, PA 17257-0152 USA

In respect for the scholarship contained herein, the acid-free paper used in this book meets the guidelines for permanence and durability of the Committee on Production Guidelines for Book Longevity of the Council on Library Resources.

For a complete list of available publications
please write
White Mane Books
Division of White Mane Publishing Company, Inc.
P.O. Box 152
Shippensburg, PA 17257-0152 USA

**Library of Congress Cataloging-in-Publication Data**

Monte, Emily C., 1953-
    The lost sword of the Confederate ghost : a mystery in two centuries / by Emily C. Monte.
        p.    cm.
    "This story is a collaboration, written by nine fifth and sixth graders and Barb Richstad, their teacher, at Montessori Elementary School of Columbia, [SC?]."
    Summary: After the theft of a Confederate sword from a museum in Columbia, South Carolina, three teenagers travel back in time to the burning of the city in 1865 and meet the ghost of the sword's original owner.
    ISBN 1-57249-132-9 (alk. paper)
    1. South Carolina--History--Civil War, 1861-1865--Juvenile fiction. [1. South Carolina--History--Civil War, 1861-1865--Fiction. 2. United States--History--Civil War, 1861-1865--Fiction. 3. Time Travel--Fiction. 4. Ghosts--Fiction. 5. Mystery and detective stories.]    I. Title.
PZ7.M76345Lo   1998
[Fic]--dc21                                                              98-20332
                                                                              CIP
                                                                              AC

This book is dedicated to all the past, present, and future students of the Montessori Elementary School of Columbia.

 CONTENTS

# AUTHOR'S NOTE

Although much of the historical information is accurate, I rearranged the city of Columbia, South Carolina a bit, and those of you familiar with Columbia geography will notice the changes. The State Museum, a fabulous place, fills almost half of an old textile mill, and the history exhibits are on the fourth, rather than second floor. I just didn't think our thief could haul himself four floors up the ventilation system! Therefore, other descriptions of the museum are adapted from the real thing. I also rearranged the Confederate Relic Room, which became the Confederate Archives in the story. And the Confederate exhibits are on the ground floor, not upstairs as I described. The docents at the Confederate Relic Room really are Civil War experts and full of great stories, but Mrs. Jacobs is entirely fictional! The cemetery that is really supposed to have doors leading to the tunnel system is St. Peter's Catholic Church, but I used the location of Trinity Episcopal Cathedral across from the State House and called it a Baptist Church! And a small note of pronunciation—"Gervais" is loosely pronounced "Jer-vay."

I would like to thank Chief Rachel Sharp of the Division of Public Safety at the South Carolina State Museum for her tour "behind the scenes," her talk about museum security, and her stories of "Bubba," the museum ghost. You may recognize Chief Sharp as Chief Blunt in the story! I'd also like to thank Ms. Nancy Higgins of Public Information at the museum for arranging our meeting with Ms. Sharp.

Many of the rumors and descriptions of the tunnel system were taken (some changed and fictionalized) from a fascinating story, "Unearthing History," in the November 1991, issue of *THE POINT*, an alternative newspaper. I'd like to thank the staff of *THE POINT* for providing me with an archival copy of this article. And Mr. Henry Jackson in our story is fictional, although we do have a "Trolley Man" in town!

Many thanks, also, to Officer Richard White, who gave us a thorough and entertaining tour of the Columbia City Police Department and became Officer Black in our story, Rick and Nyna's father.

And I'd like to give special thanks to Ken Richstad, who spent hours editing this story and improving it.

This story is a collaboration, written by nine fifth and sixth graders and Barbara Richstad, their teacher, at the Montessori Elementary School of Columbia. The students are: *Blake Carlton, Alexis Cornman, Marti Dennis, Daniel Gordon, Tyson Graham, Roger Keane, Nicky Naar, Kenny Richstad, and Lee Young.* All these people are me:

Emily C. Monte
April 22, 1995

# CHAPTER ONE

## The Shadow

---

A shadow, outlined by a thin moon, crept along the banks of the Congaree River near the South Carolina State Museum. The night air was warm and muggy, and the mosquitoes were biting. On the slippery riverbank the shadow's shoe sank deeply into the mud. He muttered a curse that shook his wiry frame, but kept moving towards his destination.

"There's my way in," the shadow whispered. He set a nylon bag of street clothes down behind an old gnarled oak tree. "Let's get the children to bed and go lookin' for dinner," he said with a satisfied whisper as he disappeared into the riverside.

Twenty minutes later he was inside the museum. He pushed open a small trap door, brushed tiny bits of gravel off his form-fitting black clothes, and agilely pulled himself up into the narrow space between two walls. One wall, he knew, was the original building wall, and the other was a movable wall installed to hide part of the ventilation system from visitors' eyes. To the unknowing eye, there appeared to be only one wall. "Lucky for me the museum kept this old duct work for its historical value," he thought. "Without it, I'd never be able to get past all the security. This place is like Fort Knox! The guards take 45 minutes to secure the place, setting all the ray span motion detectors and contact door alarms, and patrolling the exterior of the building. At least the alarms are so sensitive that even the guards have to station themselves off the floors. That gives me time to race to an exit once I've made my hit."

The shadow checked the pouch he wore slung over his belly. The weight was comforting, as if the success of this venture were stored there.

Knowing that there was no one on the other side of the movable wall, he unscrewed the access panel of the ventilation duct and squirmed inside. Bracing his arms against the sides of the duct, he pushed himself up until his feet were secured against the reinforcing ribs inside the tube. Slowly he pulled himself upwards. "Good thing I've done some mountain climbing," he thought. "This reminds me of a rock chimney. I'd hate to do this for a living, though. My old bod couldn't do this very often."

A long, slow time later he reached the horizontal duct work that hung from the ceiling of the second floor history exhibit hall. He stretched out, panting soundlessly. When he'd finally caught his breath, and his strength, he pushed up his sleeve to read the glowing dial of his watch. Still dark at 5:30 a.m., as the guards were changing shift and preparing to deactivate some of the alarms before opening the museum later in the morning. A perfect, slightly confused time for a little disturbance.

The shadow slithered easily along the pipe, turning left at the junction he knew would take him to his destination. He stopped again to regain his composure, then unscrewed the vent grill that hung above the museum floor. It thumped on the carpet beneath him, but he didn't care, knowing there was no one to hear and no motion detector aimed at that particular small section of exhibit space.

He grinned down at the dimly lit space and muttered, "Money, money, money." If there was one thing he needed, it was money and a lift out of a dead-end job. The shadow would even pull a crazy job like this one! Imagine, some fool wanting a *sword* stolen. Still, he was getting paid, and paid handsomely, so he wasn't bothered.

"Here I come!" Feet first, he lowered himself till he hung by his fingertips from the pipe. Then he let go, landing toes first, with ankles and knees bending expertly with the landing. "Poof!" the breath blew out of him. The shadow stared briefly at the sword in the glass case, assuring himself of the one he wanted, third sword on the left, hanging on the back wall of the display case, gleaming brass cross bar with a squirming snake knuckle brow joined to the eagle head on the pommel.

The shadow pulled the pouch over his head and hefted the three-pound lead ball inside. Rearing back, like a shot putter at the Olympics, he charged, smearing a faint trace of riverside mud on the carpet.

The glass shattered.

WOOOOOWOOOOOWOOOO!!! Alarms wailed everywhere. The shadow grabbed the sword and ran for the stairs, knowing he had 45 seconds before the first guard could reach the sword case. Of course, other guards could intercept him on the way down, deliberately or accidentally, and there was no way he could anticipate their movements. But he didn't care how many alarms went off now. All he cared about was getting behind that movable wall and down the trap door before anyone saw him. He leaped down the shallow brick stairs three at a time, grabbed the railing to swing himself around, slipped, and caught right up against a startled guard! Eye to eye, the shadow's masked face stared in the dark at the soft, gray-bearded face of the guard. A moment passed.

"Move!" yelled the shadow, pushing the guard away and racing into a wide hallway where the sound of his footsteps was suddenly lost on the carpeting.

"Down the hall!" the guard called to the others converging at the bottom of the staircase. They raced into the shadowed hall to see . . . nothing.

"He's just disappeared!"

"He couldn't just disappear! Check every corner, every closet. He's got to be somewhere close!"

But they found nothing.

A short while later the thief was on the riverbank again. Although the sky was beginning to lighten there was still darkness to hide in down along the river. The water ran high from the summer's storm. "I'm glad I escaped the storms," the shadow thought. ESCAPED! He felt a surge of relief and joy! He had pulled it off! He stripped off his clothes and pulled a pair of jogging pants and sweatshirt out of the nylon bag he'd hidden there. Looking like your friendly neighborhood jogger would not get the thief far at this early hour with all the police converging on the area, so he decided to wait out a slow hour until full daylight. He lay back and listened to all the sirens of the city police, the state law enforcement agency and crime lab trucks, and he chuckled. He brought the sword in front of him. The sword looked nice, but why would anyone want it lifted? There was a small weapons' black market, he knew, but the price would be far less than what he was getting paid for this night's work. Not his problem—as long as he got paid, he didn't care what happened to the sword.

Gazing at the sword, and wondering about its origin, the thief suddenly got a chill. He put the sword down quickly. He was no scholar, but knew when he was messing with something he couldn't handle.

Watching the beautiful sky and the late stars fade brought him to morning. He hid the sword carefully where he knew only he could find it later when the initial excitement had died down. He jumped up and jogged off the riverbank and onto the bridge. He felt energized and free and almost flew to his car. The thief pounded across the bridge to the Amoco station where his car was parked. He looked at his old gray sedan. "I need a better car for a better thief!" he said as he thought about what kind of car he'd get from this job. The car sputtered to life as he dreamed about Corvettes. The thief congratulated himself as he left. "A fine job, a fine job, indeed. Sure beats working nine to five!"

# CHAPTER TWO

## The Gervais Street Bridge

Time passed slowly on that hot July morning. I stared lazily at my best friend, Nicole Baxter. As she patted her short black hair she looked longingly over at the baseball diamond. She got up and stretched her long legs. Her legs were just like the rest of her body—sleek, strong and athletic.

"Hey, Ricky, ya wanna play baseball, or what?" Nicole asked.

"Nah, we played that last week," I replied. I really didn't feel up to getting hit in the face with a baseball today.

As if reading my mind, Nicole asked, "It's not like you'll get hit in the face or something."

My sister, Nyna, drove up in Mom's old Taurus station wagon. She rolled down the window and through her thin pink sunglasses I saw her bright, teasing eyes.

"Hey, Twig!" she yelled.

"My name's not Twig!" I yelled back at her for the ten billionth time.

She took off her sunglasses and glared at me. "Whatever. Hop in. Let's go for a ride. Now that I've got my driver's license and can haul you guys around,

*6*

why don't we go down to the river by the Gervais Street Bridge?"

"The Gervais Street Bridge?" I asked.

"Yeah, you know, over by the museum."

"I know *what* bridge. But why there?"

"It's hot. We can swim, or take the canoe, or whatever. At least it's something to do, and the river's a lot closer than driving all the way out to the lake."

"Yeah, okay. But I bet you think you're going to run into some cute guy from the high school, or something."

"Oh, come *on,* let's go."

Nicole and I hopped in the car and we started across town. Ten minutes later I saw the bridge ahead of us. It was a flat concrete bridge with concrete railings and old-fashioned green lampposts along the sides, that had been recently renovated to preserve its historic appearance. This bridge was the oldest along the river near the city, built after the original wooden bridge had been burned at the end of the Civil War to slow down General Sherman's troops as they entered Columbia. Its four lanes were so narrow and crowded that Mom always used a different bridge if she could. A narrow sidewalk ran on each side of the roadway and during early mornings people still fished off the bridge, although because of the traffic, most people now made their way down to the flat, muddy bank just south of the bridge where generations of kids, families, teenagers, canoeists, and down-and-outers had worn an informal boat landing. The bridge was almost at the fall line, the geographic barrier between the upcountry rapids and rocks and the low country slow, wide river. The Congaree River began right there at the bridge where two smaller, rockier, more rapid rivers joined. Just north of the bridge, on the east side, was the spillway for the Columbia Canal, another good fishing spot, where traders before the Civil War by-passed the rapids, and on the bank above that stood the South Carolina State Museum, housed in part of a huge old brick textile mill, the first hydroelectric pow-ered mill in the world.

We saw the State Museum on our right as we turned left across traffic onto an asphalt road leading down to a rutted dirt track used by canoeists, fisher-men, and down-and-outers. Nicole waved towards the museum and yelled, "See you after work, Mom!" Mrs. Baxter works in one of the preservation rooms restor-ing textiles and fabrics given to the museum for dis-play. Her present project involved a rare, old regimental flag from the Civil War found in someone's attic and donated to the museum by a Confederate colonel's great-grandson.

"Oooh, that reminds me. We're supposed to pick up Dad at the police station at 5:30. I'll never get to drive the car again if we forget to do that!" said Nyna. Dad's a police officer for the city. He usually works the 11:00 p.m. to 7:00 a.m. shift, (and says he likes it 'cuz there's more excitement at night!) but today had some desk work to catch up on. Dad's an energetic sort of guy and about the total opposite of me. He'd never get hit in the face with a baseball. He'd catch the ball, hurl it to home plate and get everyone out. I always think his job must be kinda fun, especially when he gets to ride horse patrol at city events. If I did that, I'd fall off the horse. He's easygoing, and we get along pretty well, even if I can't play ball, but I sure didn't want to forget to pick him up at the station after he's pulled a double shift.

We parked the car and walked down the track to the water. The path was wide enough for a truck to back down, but rough with thousands of small rocks. The water hit softly against the muddy bank. Trash littered the bank. Nyna tipped over a rusted bait can.

More than a dozen empty beer bottles dotted the weeds like poorly concealed Easter eggs.

"I wonder why they didn't invite us to their party?" Nicole asked jokingly.

The stone supports of the Gervais Street Bridge arched over the Congaree where the two smaller rivers joined and where the canal water rushed out of the spillway to join in like another faster-moving river. We tried hiking towards the bridge, about a hundred feet away. First, we just tramped through the underbrush that grew right to the water's edge, but soon there were so many tree limbs dipping into the water that scrambling over them became a real trial. And when the mosquitoes became too pesky (which was quickly!) and the rustling noises in the dry leaves reminded us too clearly that we were in snake territory, we waded into the river. The water, though warm, was a heck of a lot cooler than the air, but the muddy slime on the river floor squished right over the lip of my sneakers and into my socks. Soon we tired. Before we'd gone more than a few dozen yards up the river we'd had enough and turned back.

We regained the path and walked to the car, silent for a while.

"Well, what are we going to do now?" Nicole asked, scratching at a mosquito bite as she slid into the shotgun seat.

"What time is it?" I whined from the rear.

"5:30!"

"We better get Dad!" I said. We drove in silence the whole trip to the police station where my Dad worked. These hot, humid summer days were always hard. All I ever really wanted to do was stay in the air-conditioned house and play video games or watch movies. And an hour fighting heat, mosquitoes and squishy slime was enough to remind me of that.

We drove around the block a few times before finally finding a parking space by the police station. The municipal court building, old jail, a Baptist church, and the police station shared one block with only limited parking on three streets, and one side was totally reserved for the police patrol cars. When I was a kid I used to brag at school about my Dad, a city cop—but now, whenever I see the drab headquarters, I just get embarrassed and angry that the city never gives the police department the financial support it needs for the building, equipment, more officers, or salaries. Of course, Nyna and I hear our dad's complaints all the time. But he loves being a police officer. Walking towards the entrance I thought of the "Beverly Hills Cops" who work in a fancy, spacious headquarters with all the latest technology just busting out of their offices. Not Dad. I pushed through the glass doors, glanced left to the case of trophies for police Olympics and marksmanship, and as always paused to see the plaques commemorating two officers killed in the line of duty. Their badges were displayed, and that always reminded me that my father, too, could be the one whose badge was in that cabinet.

"Hey, Officer Blevins," I called to a cheery woman on the other side of the glass partition. She was hiding a cigarette below the counter. "I'm here to pick up Dad. And when are you going to quit smoking?"

"He'll be right with you. And probably never."

My sister and I had grown up knowing so many of the officers that many of them were like aunts and uncles. We always teased Officer Blevins about her smoking 'cuz her answer always told us what kind of day she was having. On a good day she'd tell us she was planning to quit tomorrow, or next week. But on a bad day she'd tell us those cigarettes kept her sane and she'd never quit, at least till "kingdom come"!

I could see Dad coming down the hall, grinning and joking with the other officers he passed in the narrow hallway. One guy was so big, they practically had to turn sideways to pass. Dad's a small-boned man, but keeps in great shape doing police training and martial arts. He tried to get me involved in karate, too. But I never wanted to hit anyone, or get hit myself. Dad's dad, my grandfather, was also a city police officer until he retired. He was in the army in Korea, and met and married my grandmother there. So Dad's half Korean. I wonder if he could have gotten a job as a city police officer twenty years ago? Nyna looks a bit Korean with her smooth skin and broad cheekbones. Mom says she looks "exotic" but I think that's a total exaggeration.

"Bye, everyone!" my Dad yelled towards the front desk. We heard a chorus of goodbyes. He buzzed through the security door to the waiting room where we were sitting. Everytime I see him step through that door I feel a thump of pride in my chest. He looks so good in his uniform! His name tag proclaims "Sergeant Richard Black." I'm named after him, and would like to be a police officer, too. Nyna says I'm too much of a wimp. But I resent that!

"Hey, Dad, what's that?" Nyna asked, looking at the radio-like thing Dad had under his arm.

"It's a police scanner. I want to keep up with some of the calls coming in. This one's not being used now, so I'm going to keep it at home for awhile. When we get it home I'll show you how to operate it—you'll find it pretty interesting."

We stepped out the door and crossed the street. We all piled into the car. Dad stifled a yawn. "How about some ice cream before we head home?" he suggested. "I need a sugar hit, and I've got some great new "fun at the police department" stories for your listening pleasure."

No one objected. Next stop, Adriana's Gelateria, our favorite ice cream and coffee (for the folks!) shop.

# CHAPTER THREE

## Getting Involved

We settled around a small table at Adriana's—I started in on eating my favorite kind of ice cream, coffee and chocolate, and Dad started in on one of his stories. Police work is serious business, as everyone knows, but Dad and his buddies are always telling wild stories. Some of the stuff is just crazy, but some is serious, just made funny by the way the officers tell it. Sometimes I think, "Wow! That was scary! Or dangerous!" But maybe when the danger's passed, they can make funny stories out of it. Dad always says he loves the excitement of police work. And we always accuse him of doing it just so he'll have good stories to tell. I bet he's planning the story even while he's chasing the guy with the Bowie knife.

This is how he starts. "My partner and I were staked out watching for a person we suspected of selling drugs. Then we saw a short man and a tall man. The short man sold some crack cocaine to the tall guy, and was so busy counting his money he didn't even notice us. The buyer kept urging the dealer to leave, because he had noticed us, and as soon as the dealer was finished counting his money he took off, walking fast. But, the buyer walked right up to the patrol car, and dropped the drugs on the ground—*right in front of us*! Was that dumb or what? And that was about the easiest arrest I ever made! And the dealer went to a friend's house and told her, 'You gotta hide me! The cops are after me!' The woman looked up and saw about 10 policemen converging on her house, and yelled, 'You can have him! I don't want him in my house!'"

Now, licking pistachio nut ice cream off his spoon, he said, "This morning one of my buddies jumped out of his patrol car to question a suspect. They started to scuffle, but all of a sudden the suspect looked up and yelled, 'Hey officer! Your car's rolling down the hill!' My buddy had forgotten to put it in gear! Reminds me of the time I was dragging a guy to the car and realized I'd locked my keys in the car!"

"But you won't believe what happened last night! Someone sneaked into the State Museum and stole a Confederate-era sword and got out without even a fingerprint left behind. It happened at about 5:00 this morning, just when the work shifts were changing. That added to the confusion. Apparently the thief was already in the museum, because that place is as secure as Fort Knox, and none of the alarms went off until he made a run for it after breaking the glass case with a lead ball. SLED was all over the place in minutes, but as far as I've heard, doesn't know how he got in."

"I wonder what your Mom heard at work today?" I exclaimed to Nicole. "I bet the place is buzzing with news."

"Yea, I bet it is. What's SLED, Mr. Black?" Nicole asked.

"That's the South Carolina Law Enforcement Division, a state agency. See, the museum is under the jurisdiction of state law enforcement, not us city folks. We'll hear most of what's going on, but won't be involved in the investigation. Besides, SLED's got better facilities, a bigger lab, more computer hookups.

"Hey, time to go, kids. Mom's probably wondering where we are. And now that I've had dessert, I'm ready for dinner!"

On the way out Nyna collected a stack of newspaper sections left on the other tables. "Hey, check this out!" she said as we climbed back in the car. We looked over her shoulder and saw the museum theft article on the front page. Nicole and I read the article aloud from the back seat.

"I bet we could figure out who stole the sword!" Nyna proclaimed.

"You gotta be kidding," I said as Dad chuckled.

"Sure, why not?" Nicole chimed in. Those SLED agents can do all the fancy fingerprints and computer searches, but I bet we could get more information from my Mom and the museum gossip than any of those Rambo guys. And it had to be an inside job, since the guy was probably there all night, waiting."

"Hey, I object to this Rambo business," Dad pointed out. "You wouldn't even notice a SLED agent unless he were wearing his coveralls. They're usually in plainclothes, and could just be your next door neighbor! Remember I used to be on the Special Weapons and Tactical (SWAT) team, and I'm just an ordinary guy!"

"Yeah. And I object to the assumption that the thief is a 'guy.' He could be a she!" I said.

"Okay, okay. So the female thief is going to be caught by my neighbor, the SLED agent. I still think we have as much a chance of figuring out 'whodunnit' as the police," said Nicole.

"You must be having a more boring summer than I thought, Nyna! Too bad you won't be old enough for a job for another year," Dad said, still chuckling.

"I think it might be kinda fun to follow the story, anyway," said Nicole. "We don't have to try to solve it, but we could try to keep up with the investigation.

You know, keep a scrapbook of newspaper articles, talk to my mom, maybe get your dad to let us know what the SLED people are coming up with . . . ," Nicole added.

"No way. Never. We aren't playing some stupid Hardy Boys game. I'd rather play baseball!"

"Ah come on, Rick. We aren't being serious. We just thought we'd poke around at the museum, maybe get Dad to tell us what he knows, and just see where it gets us. We haven't got anything better to do. Besides, think of it as educational—we'll practice all those 'thinking' skills the teachers preach to us. And I thought the Civil War was kind of a hobby of yours, so this should be right up your alley." Nyna would make a great politician. You agree with her even if you're not sure she knows what she's talking about.

"Okay, you got me," I capitulated. The middle of a hot summer really was pretty boring. I decided that even playing Hardy Boys would liven it up. "But only ordinary poking around. No dragging me into strange places. And we'd better get organized. I've got a scrapbook we can use for storing information about the case. Let me get it and meet you out at the hammock. We can start by putting the newspaper article in, then maybe interviewing Dad and Mrs. Baxter."

"Good luck, you deputy detectives," called Dad as he left the car for the back door of our house. "Maybe this week I can finally give you that police department tour you've been asking about. You won't get much information about the museum theft, but you'll get a general idea of how we operate. And I've been promising to take you around there since January. So this'll work out fine. Just remember not to do anything stupid. Don't go poking around where you shouldn't."

Nyna's eyes shone wistfully. But the whole idea of playing detective was kind of a joke. Nobody would really tell us anything. And we sure couldn't do any real investigation. But what the heck, it'd make a good game.

Half an hour later we met out in the XXX-large Pawley's Island rope hammock, to drink iced tea, all of us swaying and swatting mosquitoes and listening to the cicadas start up their evening choir. Mom came out to water the plants and pick up our tea glasses. She knew better than to trust us to bring them to the kitchen. We told her what we were doing.

"I'm a teacher," she replied, "and don't think that'll help you with your case, unless the thief needs to be taught a lesson!" Nicole cracked up, but Nyna and I groaned. Mom and Nicole are real buddies, because Nicole laughs at all her jokes. Sometimes they get laughing so hard Nyna and I just leave. Except that Nicole's skin is a deep, dark black and Mom's a frizzy-headed blond, Nicole seems more like Mom's daughter than Nyna does. In addition to their shared sense of unfunny humor, they're both tall and athletic. I got Mom's height, but some unknown ancestor passed on his clumsiness to me. And Nyna is Dad's clone, with a small, graceful body, and smooth Korean skin.

After Nicole and Mom finally stopped laughing, Mom added, "But here are some ideas. Tomorrow, why don't you ask Nicole's Mom to tell you what she learned over at the museum, then go check out the 'scene of the crime.' I'm sure they'll have the display area open again, as soon as the police are finished there. And find out more about the sword itself. Maybe that will tell you more about who would want to steal it, and why."

"Thanks, Mom. Okay, gang. Let's make a list of what we have to do next," I said. "First thing tomorrow we talk to Mrs. Baxter. Then we go to the museum and check it out. Number three—we get Dad to give us all the police information he can. And number four . . . well, what do you think?"

"How about doing some Civil War research at the Confederate Archives and the State newspaper? That would give you some background information."

"Research? Yuk, Mom, you do sound like a teacher," Nyna complained.

But I jumped to the idea. "Sounds great! My fifth grade class went to the Archives a long time ago. There are cases filled with all kinds of old Confederate stuff, and the lady who runs it loves history and tells great stories. That would be a great place to spend the afternoon, even if we don't get any help with this stolen sword business. And the newspaper has a library room with computers available to the public. We can see if there have been any other thefts of weapons, or Civil War memorabilia."

I turned to the next page in the scrapbook and added a title, "SUSPECTS." "We have to keep a list of suspects, too," I said. "Do we have any yet?"

"Maybe just someone who would want to sell it for money?" Nicole suggested.

"Why go to all the trouble to get up the second floor of the museum where the swords are, when it must be easier to steal other things from other places. Besides, how could you sell something that's obviously stolen and being looked for by the police?" Nyna responded.

"Maybe there's a black market in town," Nicole said. "And maybe some collector will pay high prices for Civil War stuff."

"I'd better write that down as a question to ask Dad," I said. "Are there black marketeers in town and what do they trade in? That'd be a good question to ask over at the Confederate Archives, too."

"And what are the police doing?" Nicole asked. "Let's try to get that police department tour right away. It's a good place to start, and your dad's already planning on us coming."

Nicole finally went home about 10:00 p.m. I went to bed early, but couldn't sleep because all I wanted to know was who did it and why. The whole thing was kind of funny really. We kids trying to figure out a genuine mystery. But I did not have one doubt about the entire thing. I knew we could solve it . . . somehow.

The next morning we met at Nicole's house, so we could talk to her Mom. Mrs. Baxter is really sweet, and laughs at almost everything. But what is really funny is the way she laughs. She sounds like a parakeet. That morning Mrs. Baxter told us all she knew about the theft, which wasn't much more than we'd read in the newspaper or heard from Dad.

Most of the speculation at the museum was about how the thief got in. Maybe he'd stayed in the museum after closing hours, hiding away somewhere. And where did he disappear to? There were lots of rumors, but the investigators were keeping a tight lid on the facts. The security and police had been all over the museum that day. And almost everyone at the museum had been questioned, even Mrs. Baxter. She's only a part-time employee in one small department of the museum, but I guess everyone there could be a suspect. I made a mental note to put museum staff names with my suspects' list. But there must be hundreds of staff members. How did the police eliminate suspects? They asked most of the employees if they'd seen or heard anything unusual around the museum in the last week. And they spent a long time questioning the security staff, and the history curators. Hmmm, I thought . . . suspects!

# CHAPTER FOUR

## A Bit of Clay

---

We drove past the State House on our way to the museum. We hadn't really needed to talk Nyna into taking us—my sister couldn't resist a little excitement and insisted on checking out the scene of the crime with us. Burly, bearded men with wide leather belts were waving Confederate flags on the State House grounds. Thin, young, blond women with arms folded over their stomachs, and short, round, dark-haired women stood in circles around the men.

We pulled over to listen to a man yell over a bull horn, "This is our flag! This is our heritage!"

He was interrupted by an old black woman at the thin edges of the crowd who yelled back, "Yeah, keep that old rag up there. It tells the world how racist you are!"

Nicole leaned over the front seat and said, "That flag was supposed to be displayed from 1961 to 1965 to commemorate the 100 years after the Civil War. How come it's still up?"

"The flag was kept up as a way to protest the Civil Rights movement of the 1960s. But it's really a symbol of racism to many of us, not just Blacks," I replied.

"On the other side, many whites feel that the Confederate flag is a symbol of honor, that it represents

Southern heritage and the fight for States' Rights. They claim that it's not racist and does not represent or support slavery," Nyna continued.

Still listening to yells, we started to move slowly away from the protesting crowd and past the west side of the State House.

"What are those gold stars on the side of the building?" Nicole asked, full of questions.

"Those gold stars show the spots where Yankee cannonballs hit the stone wall. This State House wasn't even completely built yet," Nyna said, pushing her sunglasses over her forehead. "In 1865 Sherman's troops were moving into Columbia after burning their way across Georgia. Look down there where they placed their cannon."

We looked down the broad, straight street which gradually sloped a mile down to the Congaree River, and then rose again on the other side where some of those Yankee cannons had been placed.

Nyna drove down the street almost to the river, then pulled into a parking spot right in front of the State Museum. Wednesday mornings weren't very crowded so we had a good opportunity to inspect the museum. I got out of the car and looked towards the Columbia Canal which flowed on the bank above the Congaree. The canal had been built in the 1840s to allow cotton and other upstate produce to be shipped past the Broad River rapids into the smoother waters of the Congaree. There was supposed to be a river landing somewhere near here, where goods had been delivered and loaded. As always, when I saw the canal, I spent a moment back in time, imagining the wooden barges piled with bales of cotton and the horses pulling empty barges back upstream.

Coming back to the present we headed into the museum and decided to go straight to the second floor history exhibits where the stolen sword had been displayed. We passed the Giant White Shark model hanging from the ceiling by the entrance, and the full scale model of the Best Friend of Charleston, the train that once ran the longest track in the United States before its smokestack exploded. We climbed the set of brick stairs to end up in front of a two-sided version of Fort Moultrie. The walls of the fort were palmetto logs whose soft wood had protected the Americans by absorbing the impact of British cannon balls during the Revolutionary War. Catching our breath for a moment, we looked at the high, bricked-in windows, the heavy beams and the metal poles all around us. It was hard to believe that the museum had once been a textile mill, full of cotton dust and the rattling roar of high-speed looms.

We walked to the section of Civil War arms, past display cases of Civil War maps and the Ordinance of Secession which gave South Carolina its claim to fame as the first state to withdraw from the Union. We passed the model of the *Hunley*, the Civil War submarine that accidentally blew itself up with the bomb it carried on a long pole in front. The *Hunley* had rammed a ship and destroyed the ship and itself. The mannequins in the submarine relentlessly turned the drive shaft, around and around. I wondered if those poor fellows had to turn the shaft even at night after the museum closed down. Once I visited the museum when their mechanism was broken and they were still, and thought how glad they probably were to be able to rest.

We slowed down to look at dueling pistols from the 1820s, cutlasses, rifles, swords and pistols.

"Look at this one," Nicole said. "The card says, 'John S. Haskell of Abbeville carried this light cavalry saber. He used it to surrender Lee's artillery at Appomattox in 1865.' Imagine that!"

"And look at this one. It's a beautiful sword from 1840 with a mother-of-pearl handle and engraved golden scabbard that belonged to Hasford Walker of Georgetown," pointed out Nyna, reading from the display card.

Then we found what we were looking for, an empty spot in the row of arms.

"This is strange," said Nicole, reading the card next to the bare metal hooks. "Why would anyone steal this sword? It's just a plain old sword that anyone could have bought. The card says, 'This sword, made by F. W. Widman of Philadelphia, is typical of those soldiers bought at local military supply stores.'"

I was looking at the card explaining the missing sword that read "OUT ON CONSERVATION," and just grunted.

In the warm, stuffy air of the softly lit second floor, with recorded work chants from the nearby slave display area, Nyna and I began studying the double-plated $1/4$-inch plate glass case with locks on the bottom that had already been replaced since the thief broke in, while Nicole looked on the floor for any traces left by the thief.

I was just about ready to give up when Nicole cried, in an excited voice, "Look!"

Looking at her fingernail, which she held up, I saw a tiny bit of red mud. Then she pointed in the shadows under the case. There, stuck in the edge between the carpet and the cabinet, was a little bit of that red mud.

"But that's just dirt," said Nyna, "There could be tons of it in the museum."

I had quickly grasped what Nicole was getting at and was quick to defend her. "But why would there be mud in that little space, and do you see any other mud in the museum?"

I had read enough detective stories to know what to do with a clue. I put the mud into the plastic baggy

I had foresightedly grabbed off the kitchen counter as we'd headed out. Every detective should be prepared. You never know when you'll need to stick a clue in a plastic baggy. I probably should have brought two!

Ever the impatient one, Nicole asked, "What now?"

"Thinking about what you said, I would like to know why the robber chose this sword and not one of the fancier ones, or why not that gun? Why not steal a fancy, valuable sword, or one of historical value like the one used for surrender at the end of the war? They're all in the same case, but the thief must have deliberately picked out this ordinary one from the middle of the display," Nyna said. "We're going to have to get a picture of that sword. Maybe that will help us see what's so special about it. Do you think your Mom could get a picture for us, Nicole?"

"Sure," said Nicole as we left the sword display area. "So, what's the plan now?"

"We check everything," I said, "corners, floors, even bathrooms. There is no basement to this building, and the security guards saw him just vanish down the hall-way. No door alarms sounded. There must be a trap door in the first floor and we're going to find it."

Nyna and I met Nicole at the bottom of the stairs. "Okay," I said, "if you were a thief, where would you have a trap door?"

Nicole immediately answered, "In the most unno-ticeable place!"

"Okay. So let's check there. In the corners." We searched everywhere on the first floor but our efforts proved futile. Nicole and Nyna checked the ladies' restroom, and I looked in the men's. We walked around the edges of the art gallery, carefully stopping to look at paintings when the guard strolled by. We slipped into the small classrooms in the education area and even tried to look through all the cabinets. Luckily there were no docents there since schools were out for the summer, and we figured we could always just act like curious, dumb kids if anyone caught us. Nyna opted out of being a dumb, curious kid and waited in the lobby for us.

"I never knew detective work was so hard," complained Nicole when we rejoined Nyna later.

"Oh well, waste of a good day," added Nyna, yawning.

We stood in the lobby and discussed our predicament. "Our main problem is that we don't know how the thief could have escaped without using a trap door. And we haven't found a trap door, so our only clue is a little mud," I said.

"Let me see that mud," Nyna said.

I pulled out the plastic baggy containing our only clue out of my pocket.

Nyna looked at it closely. "I'll volunteer one piece of information. It's not plain old mud. It's red clay."

I studied the contents of the container carefully. Nyna was right. It was red clay.

"Good Lordy," I said. "Where did this come from?"

"It must have come from somewhere else outside," Nicole remarked.

As we left the air-conditioned museum through the wide glass doors we passed another security guard. Could one of them actually be involved? Maybe a guard had helped the thief avoid the alarms and security, or looked the other way while he slipped out?"

As we left the building, we were blasted by hot humid air. How did the mill workers ever survive here? We walked away from the river to the east side of the building and found an annex about a third the height of the museum. A red metal ladder was bolted onto the old brick wall that serviced the roof of the annex.

Farther up we saw a number of bricked up windows, interesting, but not helpful. We walked around to the other side of the building onto a dirt and gravel parking lot. There was a patio intended one day to be developed into a cafe, but at present the area housed a mess. The place looked liked it probably turned into goopy mud after a rainstorm and it was bordered on the canal side by scrub bushes and litter. Piled in the weeds were the metal trusses of a dismantled bridge. I sure didn't want to trudge through that tangle—the first things I thought of were rats and snakes. Behind, but connected to the back of the mill building, stood low and burned-out brick extensions that at one time might have served as storage rooms or garages. Despite the sun I felt creepy.

We walked back towards the front parking lot. The sun seemed brighter out where everything was clean and well-tended. Just to the west side of the lot was a small manicured hill which ran down to a chain link fence along the canal. A small brick power plant building stretched across the canal. We slipped down a few feet of eroded mud to wooden steps that led to the sidewalk along the fence. Right where the fence began we discovered a worn path partly hidden by small trees. We walked down that path a dozen feet or so and stood watching the smooth surface of the canal flow swiftly by.

"What if the thief came down here to the canal?" Nicole asked.

"What would he do? Swim across? He'd have been seen for sure. And there's not enough cover in this brush to hide. Just litter and junk." I rubbed my toe futilely in the mud.

Suddenly I slipped and fell down to land face to face with what we really needed.

"Nicole, Nyna, look at this!" I said.

Nicole gasped, "Red clay!"

"Just like the kind Nicole found under the case!" Nyna said, crouching down by my face.

"Exactly," I said.

"So the thief could have come here. Or somewhere along the canal. How can we get over all this chain link fence? There're sections of it everywhere. I can't even figure out where it goes or where it connects. The thief would have had to know the whole layout if he were going to get through. And that still doesn't explain how he got across the parking lot without being seen. Or what he did once he got here. There's no bridge across the canal till you get up to the park. The park's at least a quarter mile up the canal, and the canal itself is about 90 feet across with a swift current. He couldn't swim with the sword, and he'd probably be swept into the power plant spillway before he could get across."

Nicole and I nodded in morose agreement with Nyna and stared off across the water.

The first thing I noticed was the quiet. Not just quiet, but silence. We were right by a busy city street, but the traffic noise disappeared. The sounds of men working at the power plant stopped. The normal sounds of summer insects and rustlings of birds or squirrels in the brush stopped. Only the sound of the canal water moving remained. And that sound grew louder. The air grew a little cooler, and drier, and dimmer. Not misty, but more opaque. I looked at the girls. Their faces were still, and frightened. I wasn't imagining this.

Across the canal bank we saw someone scrambling through the bushes, then in the distance heard gunfire and great booms. Smoke choked the air; the bridge was burning. A young man appeared briefly, holding onto saplings to keep from slipping in the mud. He scrambled up the slope, then looked across the canal at us. He looked terrified, but not by us. His mouth hung open in exhaustion, a sparse beard clung to his thin cheeks. In that long moment that we stared at each other I saw his clothes, and a chill slithered up my spine. He was wearing a gray wool army jacket, torn up the arm, with a canvas bag across his chest. The short stiff collar and cap identified the jacket unmistakably as a Confederate war uniform. His gaze lost its terrified look and he straightened up, now looking at us sadly. He rubbed his right hand up and down his thigh, up and down, up and down. And he faded slowly away.

# Chapter Five

## The Lost Sword of the Confederate Ghost

---

We stood there, stunned. As usual, Nyna regained her senses before Nicole and I did.

"Everybody to the car. It was probably just our imagination," she said. I shrugged my shoulders doubtfully, but started following Nyna and Nicole, who were already walking up the path.

"That was crazy!" said Nicole, as we picked our way through the tall grass and scratchy weeds.

"I agree," I said. I was so immersed in thought about what we had seen that I was slow to notice that we could hear the hustle and bustle of traffic again as we rode off. I was quite shaky the rest of the evening, as was Nyna. Our parents noticed we were unusually quiet, but nothing they tried could loosen our tongues.

The next day we didn't get back together again until late morning. The events of the previous day must have worn us out.

"But why would anyone want to steal that sword? It would be easily recognized if the thief tried to sell it and every collector in town would be instantly suspected," Nicole asked. We had been speculating about why anyone would want the sword. As we went round and round, I made a suggestion. "Let's go see Mrs. Jacobs at the Confederate Archives. Remember her,

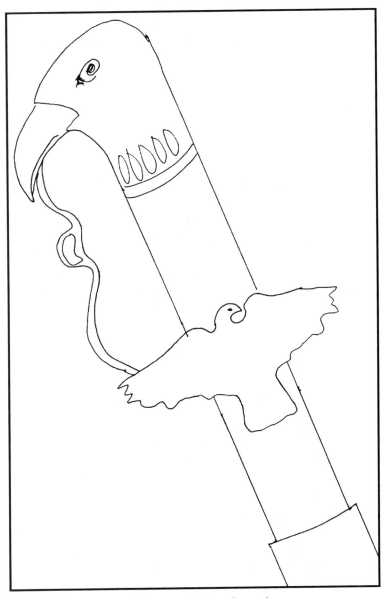

**Hilt of the Stolen Sword**

Nicole? She's the director and gave our class a great tour there last year. She seemed to know everything about the Civil War, and was pretty friendly. Maybe she'll know something about the stolen sword."

After lunch, we drove to the archives, a small cube-like stone building surrounded by a high stone fence at the corner of the old university campus. We could see the building waver, the air was so hot. We parked, got out and walked into the lovely, air-conditioned building. Turning left, we climbed a set of steps to the upper gallery and knocked on Mrs. Jacobs's open office door.

"Come in, come in! And how may I help you?" said the woman seated at her desk. Mrs. Jacobs was a middle-aged woman my mother would have described as solid and sensible. She wore a navy blue cotton skirt and blazer, white blouse, and brown, rubber-soled shoes. I guess she wasn't really old, but looked to me like one of the older teachers at school.

"Hello, Mrs. Jacobs. My name is Rick Black, this is my sister Nyna, and friend Nicole Baxter. Nicole and I were here for a class tour last year, and thought you might be able to help us with a project we're now involved in."

"You're not doing a school project now that summer is here, are you? That would be highly unusual!" she said, smiling, as she came around the desk and walked out into the gallery with us.

"Not exactly. But we're interested in Confederate swords and artifacts and know that you have a big collection here, and tell some great stories." My flattery worked because Mrs. Jacobs laughed.

"There are more books published each year about the Civil War than any other kind of book except the Bible. We hobbyists have to specialize in very particular areas since there's so much competition! And my specialty is really photography, which was just developing then. But I may be able to tell you a little about swords and other weapons. Do you have any particular questions?"

As I listened to Mrs. Jacobs I could sense Nyna and Nicole glancing around the display cases full of Civil War memorabilia: Bibles pierced by bullets, a tooth extracted from a general, binoculars, a medical case, Confederate money, small photos, weapons of all sorts, an antebellum dress made of pineapple fibers, and an old regimental flag. The room had a hard stone floor with high, high walls that rose to an ornate, but peeling ceiling. Here and there around the room were oddly placed buckets and old towels.

Mrs. Jacobs followed our gaze. "Oh yes, it's a beautiful building. But there's no money to maintain it. We've been begging for state funds to repair the roof. The leaking is terrible, and all the rain this summer has just about destroyed the ceiling."

"A Confederate sword was stolen from the State Museum two days ago and we wondered if you might know anything about it," said Nicole, bringing the subject directly back to the matter at hand.

"Of course I do!" cried Mrs. Jacobs. "That sword was carried by one of my ancestors for the Confederacy in the Civil War! I read about the theft in the paper. I can't imagine why anyone would want to steal that sword when there are so many fancier and more famous ones. That was just a common weapon that troops bought at military supply stores."

"How much would a collector pay for a Confederate sword?" I asked. "And would a real collector buy a stolen sword? Would someone have to pay more, or less, for a stolen sword?"

"Let's see. I'm not really sure, but in my office I've got a book that will tell us," she replied as we followed her into her office. "Here it is. It's called *The*

*Confederate Collector.* Hmmm. Looks like swords go from $500.00 to $7,800.00 for this presentation sword sold at auction last year. But the sword you're talking about wouldn't cost nearly that much. It's probably worth closer to five or six hundred dollars, I would say."

"Why on earth would anyone go through all that risk for a lousy five or six hundred dollars?" Nyna wondered.

"Let me tell you our old family story about that sword!" Mrs. Jacobs said quickly, closing the book and putting it back on her shelf as she ushered us out of her office.

"A story! Great!" Nyna responded.

"Of course! Take a seat!" said Mrs. Jacobs. "Once upon a time, there was a brave, young, Confederate soldier named Jonathan Jacobs. He fought at many battles, and was brave and valorous in all of them. At his side was his trusted sword which had slain many a Yankee soldier." I saw Mrs. Jacobs's eyes grow moist and distant as she recalled her long-lost ancestor. "He fought at Bull Run, Manassas Junction, Gettysburg . . . the list is endless! He survived many a fight, and stood out till the end! He was here in Columbia when Sherman burned it. The story goes that he was separated from his fellow soldiers and got trapped on the riverbank near where the Gervais Street Bridge was burning to slow down the advance of Sherman's troops. But we don't really know what happened. All we do know is that his family never saw him again, and nothing was ever found but his sword, lying in the mud right at the river's edge.

"My granddaddy donated that sword to the museum when the collection there was first being built up. A shame, too, because he really should have given it to the archives. We're more concerned with preserving Southern history and heritage here. But no, he thought the State Museum would have better displays and better security, and more visitors. He was right, of course, but only because they have that grand old mill building and so much money." Mrs. Jacobs paused here to look at the damaged ceiling again.

"But Jonathan Jacobs's story hasn't ended yet. Some say his ghost still roams the riverbank, looking for his lost sword." Suddenly the air-conditioning in the building seemed to drop ten degrees. Even Mrs. Jacobs pulled her blazer tightly across her chest. "Of course, that's just an old story!" she finished off.

"Th-thank you, Mrs. Jacobs!" I stuttered. We thanked her as gracefully as we could under the circumstances and backed out the door as soon as we could. Before I turned I saw Mrs. Jacobs turn to pick up the telephone receiver with a curious look on her face. As soon as we were out of earshot, we started babbling frantically.

"Th-th-that thing w-we s-saw m-must have been the Gh-gh-ghost!" shouted Nicole.

 # CHAPTER SIX

## The Tunnels

---

"I still want to know why someone would steal a sword from the museum, with all its security and risk, for only a few hundred dollars. That just doesn't make sense," I said aloud as we climbed back into the hammock for a business meeting.

"Maybe the thief didn't want money," Nyna answered me. "Maybe the sword has some other value, something personal. Maybe someone's willing to pay much more than the market value for this sword. Maybe there's a black market that will pay more than these book values. Maybe, maybe, maybe."

"I wonder where we could get more information about Civil War swords and robberies of Civil War items?" Nicole asked.

"How about going to the State Newspaper building and using their computers to do a search? They store copies of every article they've ever printed," Nyna suggested.

I'm a member of the Young Writers' Staff. Ever since fifth grade I've written a dozen stories a year for publication in this special section of the paper that comes out on Thursdays. Every month we have a meeting, and at one of those meetings we learned about the newspaper archives and library and were told we could use it any time. Going there sounded like a good idea.

"Just so we're back for dinner," I insisted. Mom was cooking grilled cheese sandwiches, my favorite, and I couldn't wait to eat.

On the way to the newspaper building I was still pondering why anyone would want to steal a sword and why would he be careless enough to track mud to the scene of the crime?

We parked in the visitors' lot and walked into the large glassed-in reception area. "We'd like to use the library, please. I'm on the newspaper Young Writers' Staff," I said to the lady at the front desk. She directed us to the library and computers on the second floor.

I sat down at the desk with the extremely high-tech computer set-up and typed away. With Nyna and Nicole reading over my shoulder we scanned through long indexes. An hour later we had read about the organizational meeting of a local chapter of the Daughters of the Confederacy, the donation of the Civil War flag that Nicole's mom was working on, a three-day Civil War reenactment event at Rose Hill Plantation, and a feature series on the controversy about flying the Confederate flag at the State House. We made a copy of the feature, because after our sight of the flag protesters a few days ago, we were interested. But the other articles didn't seem to apply to our case. We also found loads of robbery cases, but nothing about thefts of Civil War artifacts.

"Hey, look at this," I said. "It's about a woman who overheard a phone conversation about a murder plot on a police scanner, recognized the voice and name, and reported it to the police!"

"That's kinda hard to believe, Rick. What are the chances of recognizing someone's voice on a police scanner? Besides, how could you pick up a phone conversation on a police scanner?"

"Easy. Cellular phones can be tuned in on the scanner if you get the right frequency. But this article is only a paragraph long, no details, just picked up from *The New York Times* . . . Maybe we can fiddle around with Dad's scanner and pick up some interesting conversations!" I said slyly. "But wow!" I screamed out, everyone in the library looking toward me wondering what three year old was roaming around. "Look at his article!" I'd found an article about rumors of an underground, pre-Civil War tunnel system from the Congaree River to downtown, passing right under the State Museum!

Nyna and Nicole read over it quickly and Nyna answered my unasked question. "This could be the way the thief escaped from the museum," she said in a puzzled tone.

"'Local amateur historian, Henry Jackson, claims these rumors of a tunnel system are true, despite the scoffings of state archivists, historians and engineers,'" I read aloud from the article. "'Henry Jackson, affectionately called "The Trolley Man," runs a sight-seeing business in Columbia using old trolleys converted to busses.'"

"Guess he's our next stop," said Nicole. "I've seen those trolleys parked across the Gervais Street Bridge, just past the museum. And I bet his office is right there."

"Great," I said. "And now for some grilled cheese sandwiches!"

So the next morning we got up early and went to find the "Trolley Man." As we turned off the street, a gray Sentra sedan pulled slowly ahead of us.

"Look at that bumper sticker," I gestured. "It's a series of Confederate flags including the early Stars and Bars of the Confederate States, and the Battle Flag with its crossed bars. That's odd, though; I'm sure that car was in the parking lot when we came out of the newspaper library yesterday. Did either of you see it?"

"Nope. Guess it's just a small world," replied Nyna, distracted by the "Trolley Man" opening his door to us.

"Good morning," the lanky white-haired man wearing overalls said cheerfully to us as we walked in. "May I help you?"

"Yes. This is Nyna and Nicole, and I'm Rick. We heard you're an expert on the tunnel system," I said to butter him up. "And we hoped you'd tell us a little about it."

"Well, you know, not too many people believe in those old tunnels. But back in the days before the Civil War, cotton was King in South Carolina. The upcountry farmers would send their cotton down the Broad River in barges, then take it around the rapids on the canal down to where the Broad joins the Congaree. Right there was a landing dock where the barges could stop to unload cotton brought to the Columbia mills, and on the return from Charleston they could load up on goods needed for their farms. The tunnels were built to provide a route to the downtown business district without dealing with the mud or dust, people and animal traffic on the city streets. The tunnels were wide enough for a mule to pull a wagon through."

"If you're so sure about these tunnels, how come other people don't agree? Can't you just go in them?" I asked.

"You know, Columbia was one of the first planned cities in the world. Washington was another, so we're in good company. But most of our architectural records, including the original plans and additions to the city before the Civil War, were lost in the fires when Sherman came through Columbia, so there's no proof of these tunnels. The canal was designed and built in the early 1820s by Robert Mills and Henry Blanding. So, my guess is that the tunnel system was part of those plans."

"Didn't Robert Mills design the Washington Monument, and a bunch of those old houses in Columbia?"

"Yes, he did. And he also designed the Bunker Hill monument near Boston, and the Treasury Building and old Post Office in Washington. He was quite a famous South Carolinian. He was innovative, too, and designed the State Mental Hospital so the patients could have sun all day. All of which makes me believe he could have, and would have, designed a tunnel system as part of the canal transportation system."

"Is there any other evidence for a tunnel system?" I asked. "It's just hard to imagine that there are tunnels under the city and no one's explored them."

"There are some other ideas. The first Columbia water works was a reservoir over in Sydney Park, right near downtown. A steam engine was used to pump water from the canal through wooden pipes held together with copper straps. The pipes would need maintenance, of course. So perhaps brick tunnels were built to contain the pipes. And some people think that whatever tunnels there may be were just designed to be storm drains to prevent storm run-off from washing out the canal dike, not to be used for transportation all the way to downtown."

"Did you ever try to find the tunnels, sir?" Nicole asked. "Where would we go if we wanted to try to find them?"

"Oh, lots of people have hunted for them. Without much luck, I'm afraid to say. Apparently the entrances were filled with sand. But if you've got the 'tunnel fever,' you might try exploring a couple of places. Try getting into the basement of the old Beck's Department Store on Main Street. There are rumors of a tunnel entrance down there. There're also rumors of steel doors leading to the tunnels from the cemetery behind Columbia Baptist Church near the State House. And, of course, a search wouldn't be complete without checking out the basement of the State House. The new stone building was just being built at the time of the Civil War and even though those plans were burned along with other records, there are acknowledged tunnels under there. But don't forget, those tunnels would be 30 or 40 feet below ground when you get to the downtown area."

"Thanks so much for all your help, Mr. Jackson. You've really given us a ton of information."

"Now it's my turn to ask the questions! How come y'all are so interested in the tunnels?"

"We're trying to figure out how someone could get in to the State Museum to steal a Confederate sword!" Nicole blurted out before I stabbed her in the ribs with my elbow. "Ouch!"

"I read about that theft. There sure are a lot of dyed-in-the-wool Confederate descendants and hangers-on who would love to own anything authentically Confederate," Mr. Jackson said, narrowing his eyes. "Good luck with your explorations. And if you find anything, let me know! Folks mostly think I'm a nutty old man with all my tunnel ideas. But I still think there must be some truth behind those rumors. Besides, stone and brick passages have been found under the State House and by the canal. When I was younger I explored one tunnel by the river, but I came to a dead end. There must be some connection, some purpose."

"Thank you!" we chorused as we left his office.

"Strange fellow," I said as we waved to Mr. Jackson through the car windows. "Seems like he's fascinated enough by the Confederacy and antebellum days to steal the sword himself, or get someone to do it for him!"

"If there really are tunnels under the city, why isn't anyone walking in and out of them today?" asked Nicole. "Are they really blocked up? Or don't they exist?"

"Guess there's only one way to find out! He said to go to four places: the old Beck Department Store, the Baptist cemetery, the State House basement, and the river. I don't get it. Why would a tunnel system lead to a cemetery?" I asked.

"I'm not sure," replied Nyna. "Maybe there was an air vent, or emergency exit. Or maybe that cemetery wasn't there then. I hope we can find out when we go exploring to all those places. Where should we start?"

"With lunch," I said.

"You're always hungry!" Nyna complained.

"I'm a growing boy!" I bragged. "And my mind shuts down without a constant supply of caloric energy at regular intervals. You need me to solve this case. So you gotta feed me."

"Are you kidding?" the girls yelled as they smacked me. Oh well, the price of a joke.

But we stopped to get gas and a snack before heading on.

"Don't we need to get permission, or something, before we go poking around in these places?" Nicole asked.

"We probably should," Nyna said. "Let's see. I know old Mr. Beck. His granddaughter was in my economics class last year and we talked to him about a marketing project we did last year. I'm sure he'd remember me. I'll call him and ask if we can explore the basement."

"And I bet I can get permission for us to explore the State House basement. I'll make the State House design or history an article for the newspaper Young Writers' Page, so it'll be an official trip," I said.

"That leaves us with the river and the cemetery," Nicole figured. "And I'd just as soon wait till tomorrow morning for the river. I've got a softball game at four o'clock, and that doesn't leave us time for exploring the river."

"So, let's head for the cemetery," Nyna said, stepping on the gas and pulling out of the gas station.

We parked on the side street next to the church. The church is a beautiful stucco building with narrow stained-glass windows and a wrought iron fence all around its churchyard. We walked through the gate trying to look like casual, curious tourists, pausing to read the headstone inscriptions and pointing, for the benefit of any observers, to the Spanish moss hanging from the live oak trees. Actually, the cemetery really is interesting, with old South Carolinian names like Hampton, and Rutledge, and Pinckney inscribed on toppling headstones. We stumbled on the uneven brick walks as we circled through the cemetery looking for large metal doors.

"Lookey here," Nicole said pointing to sure-enough-large-metal-doors grown over with grass.

I pushed the weeds aside and grabbed the handles.

"Don't!" I yelled, as Nicole took the handles from me and heaved, hard.

Inside the heavy doors was . . . sand. "That's what Mr. Jackson said!" exclaimed Nicole. "That all the entrances were filled with sand."

"Why in the world would these doors cover a bunch of sand? I mean, everything else around here is just plain old dirt," I said, scraping the ground with my foot. "Someone deliberately filled whatever hole is there with all this sand. I wonder who can tell us who, or why?"

We went in the back door of the church to the office and found the church secretary.

"Pardon me, ma'am," Nyna asked as politely as possible, "But we were just studying the gravestones in the cemetery and came across two huge steel doors. Do you know what those are for?"

"I bet you've been talking to old Henry Jackson, haven't you? He's always sending people over here claiming that there's an entrance to some tunnel system under those doors. But that whole tunnel idea is a rumor. And there's nothing down there but an old storm entrance to the church basement filled in years ago to keep tramps from sneaking in. Y'all'd do better not to listen to him." And with that she returned to her paperwork, dismissing us.

"Oh well. Nothing conclusive. Maybe that storm entrance to the church basement connected to a real subterranean tunnel. And the place is right across the street from the State House building, and directly on a line from the river, passing the museum and up to here," I speculated as we stood by the fence for a moment before heading home to make phone calls to arrange our next explorations, and to eat again before watching Nicole's softball game.

That night I set my alarm clock for 8:00 a.m. in order to prepare for our 10:00 a.m. visit to the Beck Department Store which Nyna had arranged. Then I fell straight to sleep.

"Beep, beep," was the sound my clock alarm made before I slammed my hand on it. I put on my favorite shirt, the one with green and blue stripes, and pulled on cut-offs. I called Nicole, then ate breakfast as I waited for Nyna to get up. She never likes to wake up in the mornings, an affliction I'll probably develop in a few years. At least she doesn't spend hours in the bathroom putting on makeup and fixing her hair like the characters on TV shows.

We finally headed out, glad to get away from home with the car. We sure wouldn't have been able to do all this a few weeks ago before Nyna got her driver's license. I just hoped Mom or Dad wouldn't want the car for the next few days.

"How do you do, Mr. Beck," Nyna said shaking hands with him. She sure could act grown-up when she had to. "This is my brother, Rick, and our next door neighbor, Nicole. Rick is on the Young Writers' Staff at the newspaper, as I explained to you on the phone, and is doing an article on rumors of the old Columbia tunnel system."

That sneak, I thought. Now I was going to have to write two articles for the paper, just to justify all our nosing around.

"Sure, I've heard those stories, too. And I've owned this building for 40 years and never seen any evidence of the tunnels."

"Do you think we could look around the basement and see if there are any places a tunnel entrance could be hidden?" Nyna asked.

"I guess that'd be all right. There's nothing down there, really. Just stay clear of the heating and air-conditioning units. I sure don't think this old building has anything to do with any tunnel system. And I think if there were tunnels like that under the city, someone would have found them. But why not look? I suppose the search will make a good story for you, young man."

I hate being called "young man." But I politely thanked him as I gritted my teeth and followed as Mr. Beck escorted us to the basement and handed us some flashlights to use. "For your search," he said with a straight face, although I think he thought the whole thing was funny. And just as he'd said, the basement was empty, and huge. We told him we'd check with him before we left, and then stood in the middle of that big empty place and wondered what to do. None of us had any experience searching for anything other than a missing sock, and none of my well-read detective stories seemed to apply to a real search in a real basement.

"Whew, do we have to touch anything?" Nyna asked. "I don't like these dark corners, and all the creepy crawlies just waiting to jump on us."

Actually the place was really clean, and I told myself that the exterminators probably took care of all creepy crawlies including our huge cockroaches, but nevertheless I didn't much care for this business either. "Sure you gotta touch everything," I said bravely. "How else are we going to discover the secret entrance?"

"I don't think a wall is going to swing back on a special hinge, Twig," Nyna said scornfully. "This brick and mortar just feels like any old brick wall around here. There sure is a lot of brick in Columbia. I guess the old brick works supplied everyone!"

"I didn't feel or see anything along this wall," Nicole said, turning the corner. "And I'll just eyeball behind the furnace here. Mr. Beck said to steer clear, and I don't want to get stuck back there and get in trouble. Besides, it's the same old solid brick and mortar."

We kept up our search for another silent fifteen minutes.

"Here's a shelf sort of thing in the wall here," Nyna called us over. "It's wood, but recessed into the wall. You can't see it till you get close."

I pressed on the wooden back of the shelf and felt it give a little. I pressed harder and it fell backwards! With chills racing down our back we grabbed whichever arms were closest to us. A long, long moment passed. Nothing happened. We peered between the shelves and with the basement light faint behind our heads and the flashlight beams ahead of us, we could see the opening into which the board had fallen.

"Sand," I whispered.

We pushed and tugged, but the shelves themselves were firmly anchored into the brick wall that formed the sides of the shelf. And none of us were small or thin enough to fit between the shelves. We headed up the stairs, brushing off our dusty hands on our cut-offs and congratulating ourselves on our discovery and our adventurousness.

"Mr. Beck! We found a shelf in the brick wall down there. And behind it is a space filled with sand! Do you think that could be a tunnel entrance?" Nyna exclaimed when we reached his office.

"Oh that," he said dismissively as our spirits sank. "I think that was an old storage space. We built the shelf there to keep the sand from drifting into the rest of the basement, then never used the shelf for anything."

"Didn't you ever want to dig through the sand and see what was there?" I asked.

"Are you kidding? Do you know how much it would cost to excavate that much sand? We'd have to get equipment in here, and hire people to run it, then do something with all the sand we dug out. No thanks. That'd be a useless job."

We knew when we'd hit a brick wall, figuratively as well as literally. So we gave our thanks, and told Mr. Beck to watch for his name in the news article I'd write in the next few weeks.

"The river, next stop," Nyna said.

"After lunch, you mean," I corrected. "And we have an appointment at the State House for tomorrow afternoon, right?"

After a delicious lunch of grilled cheese sandwiches ("Again?" Nicole complained), we covered ourselves with

sunscreen and bug repellent, put on hats and old ten-
nis shoes for slogging around in water and mud, stuck
disposable flashlights in our pockets, loaded the family
canoe on top of the car and headed back to the Gervais
Bridge landing. This time we were prepared.

"What do we need flashlights for?" Nicole complained. "It's too bulky in my pocket."

"It's part of a good detective's kit. Just like these
plastic bags and twists, permanent markers, and wa-
terproof pad," I instructed.

"So where's the fingerprint kit, the magnifying
glass, and the plaid hat?"

"Just shove, you two," Nyna yelled at us.

We pushed the canoe into the water and started
paddling upstream, not an easy job.

"Head for the middle of the river," I instructed. "I'll
use my binoculars to look for any suspicious areas."

"Suspicious, huh. The suspicious thing is how Nyna
and I ended up paddling while you're hanging out for
a ride!"

"I'm the one who brought the binoculars, right?
Now paddle a little harder or we'll never make it under the bridge." I bet they would have dumped me out
right then and there, but they were huffing and puff-
ing too much to care. I really didn't think we'd find
anything south of the Gervais Street Bridge anyway.
The canal ended just north of the bridge, and the area
below that, where we still were, was popular with canoeists, fishermen, and hangers-out looking for a
peaceful place to drink beer. Someone would have
found something if it were there to find.

The spillway created a pretty strong current into
the river at this point. And we had to head out into the
middle of the river to avoid it and get under the bridge
before we could get back near the riverbank.

"Okay, slow down past the bridge," I called out unnecessarily, since we (actually, Nicole and Nyna) were struggling against the downstream current. "Watch out for those rocks! Head back to the bank!" I started to get excited, I had a feeling—a tingling in my fingers and an itch on my skin—something was going to happen.

Then we noticed the sudden quiet. No more sounds of cars overhead on the bridge; no more rustlings of birds in the scrub bushes on the bank. The air turned opaque, and we heard . . .

"Oh God, where are they? How do I get outa here? I can't see a thing!"

And up on the bank ahead of us was that dirty young man in that torn jacket, crouched in the bushes and looking frantically behind him, then up the bank. The air darkened and stung our eyes with smoke from the bridge burning behind us as we rocked in the canoe, still on the river.

"Aaah!" he screamed and crumpled forward. More noises of people scrambling through the woods—and we saw other soldiers with bayonets glistening from their rifles. But the air was so dark and smoky they couldn't find the man they'd shot.

"Forget it. He's dead. Let's get up the hill before someone shoots us." And a few minutes later they were gone. The air cleared only enough for us to see our young soldier push himself up, blood and pain on his face, and lean gasping on the huge, gnarled oak tree behind him. He looked directly at us. He stuck his arm out, fist closed as if grabbing something and then waving. Then he slowly dragged himself around behind the tree and disappeared.

The air cleared; the sun and heat and humidity returned. Birds rustled in the bushes; the cars roared across the river overhead.

"Jeez, incredible," I breathed. The girls paddled frantically to the bank and dug their oars in to pull us up on the mud. In a slow line, we walked to the tree which the soldier had leaned on. It was just a large old water oak tree, fat around the middle, trailing oar-shaped evergreen leaves into the mud. There was nothing unusual around it, just undisturbed mud and decaying leaves.

I put the binoculars to my eyes and followed the path of the other soldiers up the bank. Nothing. I swept my eyes farther up the bank, and, "Hey! Look! Up there in the bamboo thicket. Is that brick?"

We pulled ourselves up the slope and discovered a brick archway, tall enough for a man to stand under with a thin stream of water draining out. "There's a wooden floor here!" I exclaimed. "Hand me a flash-light. How far can we see down there?" I shone the light down the tunnel.

"It's big enough for a mule to pull a wagon through," Nyna said thoughtfully. "But why would a transportation tunnel entrance be here? There's no dock or landing. And this isn't the canal."

"Maybe there was a landing, a hundred years ago," I argued. "Or maybe the tunnels were never completed, so the landing site wasn't either. Or the landing site on the canal was connected to the river for some rea-son. Whatever, we've gotta go in a ways and see what's there." I think excitement was making me stupid, and Nicole and Nyna resignedly followed me. The water got gradually deeper until it was ankle deep about fifty yards in, but it seemed clean. And there were no snakes or rats, that we could see, anyway. The walls turned from brick to cast iron and got narrower.

"You hear that noise, Rick?" Nicole asked.

"Yea."

"What is it?"

"Sounds like a wall of water rushing towards us."

"Uh huh. That's what I thought."

"Wait! It's okay. That sound's coming from another tunnel! Look ahead!" I shone the flashlight along the walls to another tunnel joining us at right angles. The other tunnel dropped about four feet to our level. We sloshed up to this tunnel, looked both ways, and saw light at one end of the new tunnel. Our original tunnel continued to slope upwards, drying out, and ended at a wall we could just see at the end of our flashlight beams. So we turned left. The tunnel became wider, and brick again, with granite arches and wooden floors. We finished at an entrance covered with vines and waded out into a small creek.

"Where the heck are we?" We climbed up the bank of the creek and turned back and forth trying to orient ourselves. Through the trees we could see a large, warehouse-like brick building. "What building is that?" I wondered, trying to think of all the buildings up and down that side of the river. The only large, red brick building anywhere near there was . . . "The museum!" I yelled. "That's the back of the museum! We don't recognize it because we're used to the huge windows and modern entrance way. But that old brick building there is the State Museum! We must have walked right under the canal!"

"But that tunnel doesn't seem to have any purpose. It just connects this creek with the river. Sure it goes under the canal, but that's it. It probably is just a big storm drain designed to keep storm run-off from overflowing into the canal," Nyna figured.

"Yea, but if we found this much there may be more!"

"I don't know. Someone like us could have found this bit of a tunnel and spread the whole story about tunnels all the way to downtown. Just like a fish story."

"Right now, I care more about how we're getting back to the canoe from here," Nyna said. "Wooden floor and brick walls or not, I don't want to go back through there!"

"We've got to get the canoe, and the tunnel's the only way back," said Nichole. "But, seeing that ghost on the riverbank was scary enough. I wouldn't want to run into him in that tunnel!"

GHOST. We hadn't really stopped to think about it. Maybe we didn't want to give the word any reality, or acknowledge that if we all saw him and had the same experience, then we couldn't dismiss it as a dream, hallucination or imagining. I shivered, and knew that the girls did, too. So close together that we bumped each other as we walked, we headed quickly through the tunnel and we didn't slow down or relax until we were back on the river.

"Time to go home," I said. No one disagreed.

The next day we dressed up for our appointment with the Public Safety Director of the State House. The girls wore some sort of cotton dresses, and I wore slacks. Hot for July, but I wanted to make a good impression.

"How do you do, Mr. Maynard. Thanks for agreeing to meet with us. I've been researching stories about an underground tunnel system here, and heard there were tunnels under the State House."

"Oh, those stories have been passed around for years. I think they get more elaborate every time they're told. When I was your age we just thought there was one big tunnel from the river to Main Street. Last time I heard, those stories included a whole network of underground tunnels under the city! But I can tell you, part of my job is to make sure this entire capitol building is secure, and to know every inch of it. And those tunnels in the basement were built only for drainage and storage. They go nowhere."

"Well, maybe my story for the Young Writers' Page will have to dispel all the rumors. But I still think it's a great story, and while I'm telling about tunnel rumors I can also tell about the history of Columbia and the State House," I said, trying to act intelligent and persuasive. Somehow I had to get us down in that basement!

"If you want history, I'd be glad to show you around the building. It's a fascinating place. Come on . . ." So for the next 45 minutes we oohed and ahhhed, and I took copious notes. Finally, "And now here's that basement you were so curious about."

"These sure are gloomy tunnels," I remarked as he escorted us along. "But look at those giant granite arches. They look like they were built for something more important than just drainage and storage."

"If you've been studying this building, you probably know that the architectural plans were burned in the fires in 1865. But every part of the State House was designed carefully, to be artistic as well as useful. So there's no question that even the cellar would have been built this well."

We passed through these large granite archways to a narrow brick tunnel. That tunnel then led to a dirt-covered passage that ended at a downward slope with a passageway to the surface that Mr. Maynard said opened on to the grounds above.

"So you see, that's all there is to your tunnels, folks. I can see how someone could imagine something more complex, but believe me, there's nothing."

"How many times has he said that?" Nyna whispered peevishly. The long tour was making her grouchy.

"I wonder why the tunnel just seems to end like that?" I whispered back. "It starts to slope down, then just stops. I wonder if the passageway goes on, but was blocked when they closed down the tunnel system?"

"This was probably just an escape route for legis-lators in trouble," she said loudly enough for our guide to hear. He turned and grunted a bit. I'm not sure if he thought that was funny, or if we were getting on his nerves, too.

"Thanks so much, Mr. Maynard," I said to him as we shook hands. "I certainly learned a lot. I'll get this story written up and it should appear in a few weeks. My editor from the paper will probably call you in a few days to set up a time for a photographer to come get some pictures of you for the article, if that's okay."

"Well, of course," Mr. Maynard said expansively, as he escorted us out the door.

"You sure are a brown noser, Twig. And now you have to write two articles for the paper. Maybe that'll keep you busy for a while. Personally, I'm getting sick of this tunnel searching," Nyna spouted as she stepped ahead of me towards the car.

"Grumpy, aren't we? It's not as if you're missing a date or something. And you were the one who talked me into getting involved in this thing. I was smart enough last week to know this was a stupid idea!"

"Hold on, you guys," Nicole pleaded, grabbing my arm. "We're all just tired and hot. So the tunnel search didn't really get us anywhere. It was still an adven-ture. And it sure beats sitting around swatting mos-quitoes or playing Nintendo. And Rick, I'll help with those stories."

Wow, what a friend! Nicole had a way of smooth-ing things over, and always offered to help, whatever the problem. Just then, as we reached the car, the clouds, which had been building into thunderheads all the long, hot afternoon, darkened thickly and the wind started to pick up, pushing the tree branches and swirl-ing dry leaves and twigs horizontally through the air. What had been a low rumble in the distance a few minutes ago erupted into a cracking explosion right overhead. I slammed the door as we threw ourselves into the car.

"Home, James," I ordered. Nyna laughed and put the car in gear.

# CHAPTER SEVEN

## Officer Dad

"Brring!" My alarm clock buzzed. I reached out and switched it off. I was NOT, repeat NOT, getting up early this morning.

A few minutes later Nyna came in and started fiddling with my radio. I ignored her until the all-heavy metal station blasted me out of bed.

"What did you do that for!" I screamed.

She laughed. "To wake you up, Twig. Dad's taking us on a tour of the Police Department this morning. For the case. But he worked the 11:00 p.m. to 7:00 a.m. shift and wants us to come early, so he can take us around, then come home to sleep."

"Oh yea, I forgot. Did you call Nicole?" I scrambled into my clothes and ran downstairs. As we pulled out of the driveway I saw a gray Sentra parked across the street. Gray Sentra's are as common as fire ants, but I'd never seen one on our block. As we drove away, I wondered if that car had any interesting stickers on its rear bumper.

As always, I got a little depressed when I saw the police station. It's an old flat brick building. You'd think the city would spend some money on the police. Nope.

We got buzzed through the glass doors, and right behind Dad saw Chief Healy, a slender black man with a back as straight as Dad's. Nyna says he's "elegant." But what does she know about police chiefs? They're not "elegant!"

"Good morning," he said to us as we shook hands. "Your dad is a fine officer. I hope he gives you a good tour today."

"Thank you, sir."

Dad led us down a narrow hall, waving towards a room full of paper. "The records room. Also where all reports are initially filed. We're working to get this all computerized." He stepped aside for us to enter a small room crowded with two desks, a fingerprinting table and blow-ups of fingerprints lining the walls. Through another door was an even smaller room with a bad smell, lots of cabinets marked DANGER-ACID or DAN-GER-GAS, a brown paper-covered counter covered with ink residue, and something at one end that looked like a fish bowl in an open cabinet.

"You know in the movie 'Beverly Cops II' when they do the superglue testing?" said Dad explaining the fishbowl thing. "Well, it works. We take something with, say, a fingerprint on it and run it through this machine. The superglue we drip on it sticks to the body oil in the print and makes it clear. However, the item that the print was on is ruined."

"Ooh," we chorused.

"The rest of these cabinets contain chemicals for testing—often for drugs. But, like I said before, SLED has a much better laboratory, where they would have tested anything from the museum theft: blood, fibers, hair, prints. They'd check the roof, the windows, doors. If the area wasn't contaminated before they arrived they'd even bring in a dog to 'hit' on a scent and trail the thief."

Walking down linoleum-covered stairs in a hall-way painted battleship gray we rounded a corner to come face to face with a line of FBI wanted posters tacked onto a bulletin board. "We have national computer access to information about all convicted criminals. For example, if we were involved in the museum theft, we would search the computer records for anyone convicted of a similar crime."

"And here is the lie detector," he announced as he led us into a tiny space adjoining an office. Two comfortable chairs faced each other across a large desk that nearly filled the space. A two-way mirror was set into the wall between the office and desk, and a big, flat machine crouched on the desk. "We can't use this evidence in court, but if we had a suspect in the sword theft, we might ask him whether he would consent to a lie-detector test in order to clear himself."

Just down the hall was a smelly room with all-the-way-to-the-high-ceiling wooden cabinets and cubbies crammed with an assortment of junk: empty wine bottles, filled paper bags, old clothes, pieces of papers. "This is the property room. All this stuff is evidence that's tagged and labeled and used in different cases. Dave, can you show us something?"

"Sure can," said Dave pulling a huge-bladed Bowie knife up from under the cabinet.

"Wow!" we yelled.

"And here's a sawed-off shotgun, and there's another room back there filled with cabinets, too. And lots of guns."

"What do you do with this stuff when you're finished with it?" Nicole asked.

"Some of it's saved, some burned, some tossed, and some of it's sold. You wouldn't believe what's in here. And we keep it all. That's that bad smell—vomit on clothes, old liquor bottles. That's why we have these ceiling fans going all the time!"

"What're some of the most unusual things you've had in here?" Nicole asked, again.

"I think the smallest thing we had was a bobby pin—the label was bigger than the pin! And once we had a tombstone! Somebody vandalized the cemetery and stole it!"

"Dad, I guess that means that if you'd found any evidence at the museum, like the guy's hat, or a weapon, or a bit of clay, or something, it'd eventually end up here?"

"Yup. Now in this room Officer Manning is preparing a lineup."

"Hey, kids. This is a great computer. See how it 'reads' these photos to prepare a lineup sheet. We feed it with records of suspects that match the victim's description, prepare this layout, print it, then give to to the victim to study."

"You mean you don't line them up for real any more?"

"Nope. The victims are much more comfortable looking at photos than real people in a lineup."

"Thanks, Officer Manning. Now this office is where all stolen cars are reported."

"This little place?" Nicole exclaimed as a tall woman with long, wavy hair wearing regular clothes walked out of a map-lined room made by dividing a wide hallway into cubicles. "Everything's so small and crowded. How do y'all manage to work here?"

"We love our work," replied Dad. "But the department could sure use more money! The Fire Department is getting new stations now, so maybe we'll be next for an upgrade."

"I think it's embarrassing for our city to have such a shabby police station," stated Nicole. She'd put into words what we all thought, but Nyna and I had grown up with the police department and were more used to it.

Then Dad took us quickly through an outdoor shed with old Harley motorcycles and the newer scooters used in heavy traffic, the room where warrants were issued, an old courtroom that looked like something out of "The Andy Griffith Show," the room with two breathalizer machines, and down a corridor to the old jail. Nyna and I had seen the old jail before, but Nicole hadn't, so this was for her. The place was creepy—old brick, dark, closed-in rooms for visitors and interrogation, painted concrete floors, and every door with a lock. We couldn't get into the cells, but just peering through the bars was enough. I hated going in there and couldn't wait to get out. Besides, this had nothing to do with our case.

"Come on, Dad," I said. "Time to go home."

We trailed down the long hall back to the police building and our car.

"We had a kid in last night. Couldn't have been much older than you, Rick. He was caught stealing a car, but was too short to reach the pedals, so had tied his kid brother's cardboard building blocks to his feet!"

"Hey Dad, tell Nicole the story about the time you handcuffed the policeman!" I said as we pulled away from the curb and turned the air conditioner on full blast.

"One of my more embarrassing stories! My buddy and I had called for back-up one night while we were chasing a guy around by one of the university buildings. We chased him around a corner and he'd just disappeared. Then my buddy swept his flashlight beam under the cars, and sure enough, he'd flattened himself next to the curb. He jumped up and we tore after him into a pitch black yard. Just as my buddy and I jumped him the two other officers found us. We wrestled the guy to the ground, I slapped the cuffs on him, and my buddy yelled, "You got me, you idiot!" The suspect started to squirm out and one of the other officers, must have weighed three hundred pounds, jumped on us, just like a pig pile. He knocked the wind out of me, but cuffed the right guy!"

"Sure hope you don't ever have to chase the museum thief, Dad!" I said.

# CHAPTER EIGHT

## More Suspects

"Whoa, check this out, Nicole!" I yelled into the kitchen.

The refrigerator door slammed. "What!" came the reply.

"I think we just got ourselves another suspect. Look at this guy being interviewed by the WIS TV cast."

Nicole came through the hall that went straight through the middle of her house. She had a sandwich in one hand and a canned Yoo-Hoo chocolate milk in the other. "Just check it out!" She sat and took a bite of ham and cheese. I concentrated on what the angry-looking man on the TV set was saying.

"—— mad, and I will do anything to keep this flag up. I mean *anything!* Now all you liberals out there who think I'm a racist are wrong. And you yourselves are racists because you won't let me and the majority of South Carolinians keep our heritage flying above the State House! And—"

"Now sir . . . ," the newscaster said.

The man did not let her finish her question. "This is unfair to me, and my friends, so we will be showing our support on the State House grounds all week. If anyone wants to join us, we start at noon. Look for me, John Customs, when you come. I hope to see a lot of real South Carolinians out there!"

I cut off the TV and looked at the clock. Eleven o'clock. I looked at Nicole and a silent message passed between us. We'd known each other so long that she knew exactly what I was thinking. "Wait, Rick!" Nicole called after me as I ran for the door.

"Come on, Nikki, I want to get there in time to talk to Mr. Customs before the demonstration starts."

"Wait a minute, you fool," Nicole sounded exasperated. "I remember a newspaper article you brought back from the State Newspaper. It was about this John Customs guy and some of the people who followed him or opposed him on the Confederate flag issue. Remember what your Young Writers' Staff editor says: always do your homework, first."

Nicole was right. "Oh yeah," I managed to mumble. "Well, come on. All the articles are at my house. And bring your bike, Nyna's gone."

"Race ya!" came from Nicole and we were off. Why she always wants to race I'll never understand, but as I grabbed my baseball cap I saw her flying for the door out of the corner of my eye. Not this time, Nikki. I bolted past Nicole's screen door right in front of her. I heard a loud, "Hey!" from behind, but I had a good head start, and I wasn't going to waste it. I needed every advantage I could get over my friend. She was a track and field monster. I figured that with my head start I could take her down. I figured wrong. She passed me like I was standing still. She never ceases to amaze me. Across her lawn to the side of her house Nicole ran, kicked up the kick stand on her bike and rolled it over to my porch. She jumped all the steps to my front door and wasn't even breathing hard. I stumbled up the steps, gasping for breath. "Beat cha," she said. I would have said something smart back at her, but I couldn't find the breath for it.

"That is a pretty interesting dude," said Nicole. I agreed totally. We turned off Blossom Street onto Sumter. I couldn't help but admire Nicole's 18-speed bike. It was great, especially compared to my 10-speed. While biking no-handed I was trying to read aloud the newspaper articles I'd grabbed from home. "It says here that he had five ancestors fighting in the Civil War, one of them was even at Fort Sumter when the first shots of the war were fired. His granddad was a boy during the war and saw the Yankees steal their last horse and cow which left them so destitute that his mom died. And his father died during the war, too, so he blamed all his suffering on the Yankees. And he made sure his son, and his grandchildren, knew that the Yankees had killed his parents for trying to be independent."

"After hearing that story, I can almost understand why people would want to keep the Confederate flag flying. Of course, my ancestors were slaves. But I guess most whites in South Carolina then were too poor to own slaves. So they don't understand why we see it as a symbol of racism."

I looked to the left to see construction going on at the University Library. One wall was being torn open to accommodate a new wing. That was the way I felt about South Carolina. The state and its people are changing and growing, and old issues, like flying the Confederate flag, must be torn down to accommodate new ideas. Flying the Confederate flag offends all Blacks and many Whites, and affects the state economy because other states see us as supporting a racist symbol.

We pulled up on the sidewalk and rode between the trees and statues that dotted the State House lawn. An amazing sight stopped us. A Confederate Army camp was set up under the trees near the State House steps. Men in gray wool uniforms and small caps tended fires and horses while women in hoop skirts and bonnets stirred the contents of iron kettles. Children, also dressed in period costume, raced through the camp. These were Civil War reenactors, presenting a "living history" in conjunction with the flag supporters. Right below the broad State House steps were the supporters of the Confederate flag waving banners, posters and flags over their heads. "HERITAGE NOT HATE," "WE DON'T CARE HOW YOU DO IT UP NORTH!" "GOD, GUNS, AND GUTS MADE AMERICA FREE" read the placards.

After taking in the sight of all the activity around us, we locked our bikes and set off to find John Customs. As we neared the steps we heard a chant building to a roar, "John, John John!"

"Fellow South Carolinians, we are gathered here to make a point. We WILL keep our heritage flying over the capitol building of our home! Let the spirits of our Southern soldiers and their families stay strong, for we will win!" A great cheer went up from the crowd as the flags waved wildly overhead.

"Wow! That guy really believes what he says is true!" I exclaimed. As the crowd dispersed to find shade from the glaring sun we approached to listen while Mr. Customs talked with news reporters. He talked of how he'd spent all his life in South Carolina, his upcountry ancestors and relatives, his time at the university specializing in Southern history and culture, and how he loves to call South Carolina home. Customs ended his life story with the words, "Our movement needs your media coverage, we need dramatic events to make people sit up and take notice. What I wouldn't do to prove to all of you, to the state, and to the nation, how serious we are. Our heritage cannot be dismissed by liberal do-gooders. We don't hate, we aren't racist, we just want to show that our heritage is not something to be locked away in museums and told in history books. Our heritage is living and it's real!"

"Man, he always sounds like a TV preacher, acting like he's sincere, but really just trying to prove his power." Nicole said as we walked back towards the reenactors' camp.

"But he's good. He's really good. There's something about him, though. Maybe he seems too slick, or even a little desperate to get attention."

"Let's go talk to some of the reenactors. Maybe we can learn something from them. Part of their "living history" mission is to talk to visitors, answer questions, and show their artifacts, so we won't have to promise you'll write a newspaper article about them to get information!"

"That's a relief!" I laughed as we sat down in the shade near a small tent where a man dressed as an officer and a smaller man in a shabbier uniform talked to a few visitors.

"Yes, we try to make our uniforms, weapons and tools as authentic as possible. Some really are originals. Others are copies we make or buy from sutlers, traders who follow the troops. Our sutlers are real merchants and reenactors, too. And while we're in camp we try to use as few modern conveniences as possible, although I confess I keep a flashlight and spare batteries in my tent!" Everyone chuckled politely.

"So you really use authentic weapons? Are your guns and swords Confederate-era antiques?" a woman asked. I started paying closer attention. She was asking all the right questions!

"Oh yes, many of these are real weapons from the Civil War. Some of them are from our own families. My gun, here, belonged to my great-grandfather. There's a huge market in Confederate weapons, although they're pretty expensive. Some of the reenactors are real collectors, and one man in my company is an antique shop owner down in Charleston."

"Do you all really support flying the Confederate flag over the State House?" someone else asked.

"That's our flag, ma'am!" the smaller soldier answered with a thick "country" accent.

BOOOM! A crack of thunder cut off the rest of his answer. Everyone automatically scanned the thick sky towards the west where all our summer storms come from. "More rain!" someone groaned.

"Time to go!" I yelled to Nicole as the wind started blowing. We unlocked our bikes and rode furiously across the grounds. A bolt of lightning radiated in the dark air and we ducked under the awning of Eddie's Sandwich Shop just as the rain began to pour.

# CHAPTER NINE

## Chief Blunt

---

The next day Nicole and I were sitting in her living room thinking what to do next. Still another storm was rumbling in the distance and the wind was picking up outside, scraping branches against the windows. These summer storms could be pretty violent with always the threat of hail and wind damage. But as long as I was inside I enjoyed the excitement and anticipation of the approaching storm. Outside, or in a car was scary, though, with thick rain and winds so strong they'd rock the car. The weather reports each day were a repeat of the day before—hot and humid with late afternoon and evening thunderstorms. And the storms didn't really refresh us at all, just made the air more humid. Anything left out of the protection of air conditioning was turning green with mold. Unfortunately, the local farmers were not too happy. Some years without rain burned out the crops, and years with too much rain, like this one, drowned them.

We'd already trashed the room with spilled popcorn, videos and their empty plastic boxes, and couch cushions and pillows. Good thing Nicole's mom wasn't as fanatical about neatness and order as mine. Although I guess it's really my dad who's the neat-freak. Must be that police-academy-spit-and-polish training. I picked up the remote control and flipped on the TV.

A security guard walked slowly through a darkened museum. Spooky music followed him. Out jumped a ten-foot monster and the guard turned his face to the screen and yelled. Suddenly something clicked in my mind. I snapped off the TV.

"Hey! I was watching that!"

"Is your mom home," I asked, ignoring her shouts.

"Yea, I think so. Why?"

"Let's ask her if we can get a tour of the museum security systems. Maybe that'll help us figure out how the thief got in the museum without triggering any alarms at first."

"Great idea! I think she's upstairs."

Leaving our mess behind we took the stairs two at a time and knocked on her bedroom door. Nicole walked in first and I followed. Her mom was standing by the mirror blow drying her hair.

"Hey, Mom!" Nicole yelled over the noise. Her mom just smiled and waved happily. Nicole reached over and pulled the hair dryer plug out of the socket.

"Hey, honey; hey, Rick. Need something?"

"Mrs. Baxter," I asked, "Do you think maybe you could arrange a tour of the security systems at the museum for us?"

"You planning a break in, or something?"

I smiled. That's where Nicole had gotten her sense of humor.

"Actually, you almost got that one right. We're gonna see ways the security works so we can maybe figure out how the sword thief got in."

"So you two have turned into detectives, huh?"

"Yep, you're the lucky Mother!" Nicole said.

"Sure, I'll see what I can do. I'll have to ask someone in the security department to make special arrangements for you. I know they don't usually do

Behind-the-Scenes tours for kids. Even we adults who work there have all kinds of restrictions about where we can go. We're usually limited only to the workrooms and storerooms in our department. But I'll poke around and see what I can do for you. Rick, maybe I'd have better luck if I said you were going to write an article about museum security for the newspaper's Young Writers' Page."

"Oh no," I groaned. "I've been using that excuse for everything. I'm already committed to stories about the tunnels and the State House. But sure, go ahead. Whatever it takes. And one of these days I'll actually have to write those stories!"

"Well, I'll see what I can do. Now, plug in the blow dryer and let the 'lucky Mother' dry her hair!"

The next morning I went back to Nicole's hoping Mrs. Baxter had come through. I trotted up the stoop and knocked on the door. Nicole came out with a smile on her face.

"So, Nikki, have we got a tour yet?"

"Yup. Today. And the chief, herself, will give it! That bit about the newspaper story did the trick. Let's get a list of questions made and ask Nyna to drive us over—we're to be there at 11:00 this morning."

We made up a long list of questions about what different kinds of security devices they used, the numbers and background training of the security guards, how a thief could get by the security systems, and what the procedures were immediately following a theft. We showed Nicole's Mom the list and she was quite impressed. We hoped the security chief would be, too.

Right at 11:00 we arrived, told the receptionist we were there, and went to wait in the courtyard where a display of green watermelon-looking terra cotta spheres was arranged in an exhibit called, appropriately, "Scatter."

"Hello, are you the ones that want to hear about museum security?"

We turned to see Chief Blunt, who to my great surpise, was young—younger than my parents, with short brown hair, bright eyes and a big friendly grin. When Nicole had mentioned that the security chief was a woman, I held my tongue, not wanting to have everyone jump down my throat for assuming a security chief had to be a man. But now I found out she was a young woman and not the chunky, gray-haired person I expected! This might be a great newspaper story after all! She was wearing black pants with a blue stripe down the side, crisp white shirt, some sort of insignia, a small walkie-talkie clipped to her shoulder, and a gun strapped to her belt. Except for the uniform and gun, I could see her in jeans and a T-shirt playing softball with Nicole.

"Here you go," she said as she handed us official looking clip-on tags, "You've got to wear these security passes to go into the security offices, storage areas and back halls behind the exhibit areas. But first," she continued as she led the way to the elevator, "I'm going to show you some of the security devices in the exhibits themselves. Really, our division is called Public Safety, and we deal not only with security, but with fire prevention and personal health and safety. We're a real law enforcement agency, too, not just a security office. So some members of the staff have been trained at the Criminal Justice Academy, and are authorized to carry weapons, make arrests, and do anything else a city police officer would do. Other members of the staff are security trained from private agencies."

We left the elevator, grinning at each other and fingering our tags. This was going to be great! She led us to an exhibit depicting a mill village bedroom from the early 1900s. "The amount of security depends on the type of display. This is considered a minimum security exhibit. See those little boxes inside there, against the walls on either side, just past arm's reach? There's a laser beam that crosses in front of us. And if one of us stepped inside and crossed the beam we'd break the laser beam and trip the alarm. But this alarm is not hooked to the central system: it would summon a guard from somewhere on the floor to see what's going on. And these alarms do sometimes get deliberately tripped by kids stepping through the beams."

"But couldn't you just step over the beam?" Nyna asked.

"With some you can. But there are other scatter beams that create more of a sheet, or curtain, across the exhibit, so there's no way you could step across or around it. And if you follow me over here . . ."

"Hey, is that something?" I pointed to a small grill on the wall about five and a half or six feet off the ground that looked like a miniature heat vent.

"It sure is. This is an infrared light motion detector. It's turned off now, of course. But whenever the museum's closed it's set to detect body heat movement. And see how the grill is angled downwards? That's to prevent people from trying to slip under the beam."

"Isn't there any way someone could get past this? How about if he were wearing something that didn't let out any heat?" Nicole asked.

"Well, I suppose that's possible, but not probable. He'd have to wear a bulky insulated suit and move very slowly. And why would someone go to all that trouble? He wouldn't be able to move quickly or easily. Now over in this country store exhibit is another kind of device. See that white ball hanging from the ceiling? It almost looks like part of the display and blends in with the other artifacts hanging from the ceiling. But it's also a motion detector."

She led us down the hallway and pointed out the pan and tilt cameras mounted high on the wall. "Wave!"

she said. "One of the staff in the central office will see us." We mugged briefly for our unseen audience. "And here," she said, stopping in a doorway framed by heavy fire doors, "is a more serious security device. This is a door contact alarm. When this is set the doors are closed. Anyone opening this door triggers an alarm that rings in the central office. Security guards could be here within seconds."

"Does that mean that security guards don't actually patrol around here at night? They just set the alarms and station themselves somewhere else?"

"That's right. With all the motion detectors and door contact alarms not even the guards can move around. But, depending on the security level of the exhibit, a guard must be within 15 or 30 seconds of the display day and night. Which leads us to this exhibit, a moon rock on loan to us from the Smithsonian Museums, which is protected with the highest level security. The cabinet itself is built floor to ceiling. A guard is within seconds of this exhibit at all times, there are motion scan detectors inside the exhibit itself, cameras recording everyone who looks at this exhibit, and a proximity device attached right to the rock itself so that if someone actually did grab the rock another alarm would go off."

She lead us over to a display of Civil War weapons. "Some cases are more secure than others, like the one for the moon rock. Others need special tools to open or unlock them, like this cabinet here." And sure enough, what looked like a regular set of screw holes, on closer inspection needed a special tool. "And exhibits may have a ray span motion detector inside the exhibit itself, like this cabinet where the thief stole that Confederate sword last week," she continued as we moved aound the corner to that familiar display. "The span detector means no one could cut the glass, slip a hand in around the light beam and remove the

sword. That's why the thief just smashed the glass—
he knew he'd trip an alarm one way or other and just
decided to get the sword as quickly as possible and
make a run for it. This thief apparently knew a lot
about the museum, how it's secured, and when the
guard shifts change, always a more vulnerable time in
security."

"Do you suspect a guard as the thief, then?" I
asked.

"Oh, not necessarily. There are many ways to learn
about museum security. Even the library has books
about it. All you'd need is some patience and a few
innocent questions to a security guard—maybe while
strolling your baby around the museum on a Sunday
afternoon. But there are some famous stories of security guards involved in thefts. The temptation to make
lots of money compared to a security guard's salary
could be hard to fight. At one European museum a
number of years ago, the thieves dressed as police
officers and persuaded the night staff to let them enter, then trussed up all the employees, and stole mil-
lions of dollars' worth of paintings."

We headed for the stairs on our way down to the
central security office for the museum. We passed a
security guard on his way up. He was the perfect im-
age of a guard, trim and fit looking, but he had a tight
face—not the kind of guy you'd ask for directions to
the restrooms. "Good morning, Smitty," Chief Blunt said
to him.

"Morning ma'am. Hey you kids better watch out
for this lady," he said to us. "She's the meanest lady
this side of West Virginia." We all laughed, but the guard
didn't, and Chief Blunt looked annoyed.

A few minutes later we pushed through doors with
signs saying, "Employees Only" and a picture of a hand
in a circle. We passed through hallways of exhibit parts
and got buzzed into the central office, a room filled

with computers, video screens, radio equipment, and file cabinets. Lights blinked on control panels. Chief Blunt showed us the ways that security turned on the motion sensors, door alarms, and other security devices. A computer showed the locations of all security devices in the exhibits and other areas of the museum, and could track movements from one alarm to another. We watched the video display of the floor where we'd been walking and waved at the camera, and watched other monitors scan the front entrance and parking lot of the museum.

"This is Amy." Chief Blunt introduced us to another uniformed guard in the office. "We always have two people in the office 24 hours a day. Amy's the radio dispatcher today. And here's the most important thing in the security office, the fire alarm system. Fire is much worse for us than theft, because fire destroys the artifacts."

"But what about thefts. What happens after a theft? What are the procedures?"

"Since this did just happen to us, I can tell you exactly what the procedures are! The security guard on duty here in the office immediately notified SLED, the South Carolina Law Enforcement Division, since this is a state agency. SLED secured the area and placed yellow crime scene tape around the entire area. On TV you see the crime scene area swarming with police and reporters and all sorts of people. But that's not how it really happens at all. The agents don't want to contaminate the area so very few people are allowed in, and only SLED crime scene personnel, not even me, or the city police. They looked for hair and clothing fibers, mud, fingerprints, carpet fibers, and blood samples in case he'd cut himself on the broken glass. They looked for a trail of evidence in order to determine how he got in and out of the museum. Once they'd found as much evidence as they could, they narrowed the crime scene area down to just the space in front of the museum, and we were able to open the museum on schedule. We kept extra security there most of the next day until the SLED people were finished and the glass was replaced. Then even that exhibit was back to normal. Of course, if the SLED people had needed more time they could have kept the area sealed for days. They're pretty efficient, and know what they're looking for, so they were gone within hours."

"So then what?" Nicole asked. "Is there a black market or something?"

"Yes, there are black markets for some artifacts, like weapons, coins, and of course, art. And the SLED agents would also notify pawn shops and other museums."

Just then the security office radio rattled and squawked. "There's a dead bug by the hearse on the second floor. Please call someone to the area."

We all laughed, including Chief Blunt and Amy. "Actually, bugs really are a serious problem. I know it sounds funny to hear a call like that, but we have many valuable artifacts in the museum that must be protected, and bugs can seriously damage or even destroy them. Just think what our household cockroaches do to our books!"

"Have you told the kids about 'John-Boy' yet?" Amy asked.

"Who's John-Boy?" Nicole asked.

"The museum's got a ghost," Chief Blunt said with a smile. Many people have heard him rattling pipes and moving things around. One night I was on duty here and the alarms on the second floor started going off. On the computer I could see a trail of tripped alarms, like someone walking from one end of the floor to the other, tripping the alarms as he went. And I had to go up and check! And no one was there!"

"I saw him, too," Amy added. "Or rather, I saw part of him. I was on the second floor, making sure all the visitors were gone before we turned on the alarms. I was just heading downstairs to the office when I saw a hand come through the wall. And then an arm with a torn gray uniform—boy did I hightail it down those stairs!"

"You should have seen her," laughed Chief Blunt. "She was probably as white as that ghost. And that's hard when you're Black!"

The ghost again. We'd hardly talked about our "visions" and had just about convinced ourselves that we'd imagined those scenes, and somehow spooked each other. Now he was back—a Confederate ghost in the museum. Was he the same ghost we had seen by the riverside? What did he want? Why was he appearing?

"Let me escort you around to the parking lot," the chief said gesturing to the door. "I've got a meeting to attend in just a few minutes."

As Chief Blunt escorted us out of the office to the rear door of the museum building, we stopped to look at the huge ventilation pipes suspended from the ceilings. "Do you suppose those are big enough or strong enough for a person to crawl through?" I wondered aloud. "The motion detectors wouldn't pick up that."

"Certainly," the chief replied after a pause. "Those pipes were renovated along with everything else in the building when the museum took over. They're nice and strong. Of course, they're still used, so anyone in them would be subject to the heat or air conditioning flowing through."

"Would that be dangerous?"

"Maybe uncomfortable, but not really dangerous."

She led us around to the parking lot. We passed the burned-out buildings we'd seen earlier and asked her about them. "I'm not really sure what those were originally for. Storage, probably. I do know the museum's been thinking of trying to renovate them someday. Maybe we'll learn more about them then."

I walked toward one of the entrances and peered in. "Pretty dusty and dark in here. Looks like a bunch of old brooms and buckets, and who knows what. I guess people still dump stuff in here, though. Looks like some stuff is dustier than others."

"Come on, Twig, Chief Blunt's got a meeting. This isn't a great time to play detective!" Nyna tugged on my shirt and we headed for the front.

After thanking Chief Blunt profusely for the long and interesting tour we waved to the security cameras on top of the museum and climbed in the car.

"Man, that was great," I said. "Wasn't Chief Blunt great to tell us all that stuff? We still don't know how the thief got in or out, but we've got a lot of background information, and a lot to think about."

"And we've got a lot of new suspects," added Nyna. "Even the chief herself suggested that a security guard would have the ability and the motivation, money, to either steal the sword, or give information to someone else."

"We only saw Amy and that other guard on the stairs," pointed out Nicole. "We don't know the rest of the staff, and they could all be suspects."

"My money's on that guard we saw on the stairs. He looked mean. And that joke about the 'meanest woman' didn't really sound funny," said Nyna. "I wonder if Chief Blunt suspects anyone?"

"And we really do need to check out those old storage rooms back of the museum. Someone has been back in there shoving things around. Half that space I looked at was covered with tons of dust, and the other half had the dust all knocked off. It was obvious that stuff had been dragged across the dust and dirt on the floor," I said.

"That could have been anyone from the museum— not necessarily sinister, either—maybe just someone looking for something, or looking for a place to store something," Nicole replied.

"That stuff in there was real junk, like I said, brooms, buckets, nothing important. I think we should look around there some more."

"But not now. It's past lunch time. I'm starving. And you have a few news stories you should start writing!"

# CHAPTER TEN

## Stumped

A hot sunny day began as Nicole and I sat in the large hammock with the scrapbook. Nyna was sleeping late, as usual.

"Boy, it's gonna be sweltering today. Only nine o'clock and the temperature's already up to almost 90 degrees. Mom's got the car all day and we'll probably get thunderstorms later," I complained.

So what're we gonna do today? I bet my ball game will be canceled 'cuz of the rain, and who wants to play in the heat, anyway?" Nicole groaned.

"And no closer to figuring out who stole the sword. Dad says the police haven't a clue, and for all our work, we sure haven't got one, either."

"What have we done, anyway? We've been so busy, I'm not even sure what the clues are!"

"We might as well let it sit for a while, and go for a swim at the pool."

I jumped into my orange and blue swim suit and went to grab the towel that my grandparents brought back from Hawaii. I rolled down the stairs determined to beat Nicole. I slammed the door shut, grabbed my bike and headed for the curb. Nicole was waiting, wearing a tight green and black swim suit that I'd seen her wear before. She also had a multi-colored towel over her shoulder.

"So this swim will take up the morning. What're we going to do then?"

"Try to whip up some notes, I guess. Maybe this swim will cool off our brains and help us think a little," I answered.

We biked through the university district to the city park. The huge rectangle of blue water looked cool and inviting. I dove into the pool and started swimming across. Nicole quickly dove past me and raced to the end of the pool.

"You want to race, or are you scared I'll beat you too bad?" she snickered.

"Sure, I'll race," I said, already gasping for breath.

I felt Nicole's muscular body run across the side of my body. She touched the other side of the pool just as I was halfway through the first half.

"I win," she yelled, "and you lose!" One would wonder why Nicole, of all people, would be glad to beat me, the worst swimmer in the world, in a race. Come on! We splashed and dove and generally horsed around for about another half-hour. Then I got out of the pool and headed toward my towel.

"Come on, Nicole, we have work to do." Nicole got out of the pool and put her towel around her body.

"So I'll be back at your house in about 15 minutes," Nicole said as we pulled our bikes up the driveway between our houses. I opened the door, expecting to see Nyna on the couch watching some soap opera, or something like that, but to my surprise she was still asleep. I could tell because I could hear her snoring all the way from downstairs. I went to my room and took a shower and got dressed, then went in Nyna's room hoping to wake her up. I got to the bed and shook her.

"Hey, Twig, what was that for?" she said, as if she were Mom.

"Well, um, I wanted you to help us on our mystery," I said.

"I guess so. What can that hurt, anyhow?"

"Great! Nicole will be here in 15 minutes." I went to the kitchen to fix lemonade, then carried the pitcher and glasses out to the hammock where we'd left the scrapbook before our swim.

I climbed in and started to think what all we had done. I then went into a daydream as if I were there when the theft had taken place. I guess the swimming really had cooled me off and worn me out. "I bet the thief was just hired to take the sword for someone else, because it was all done so professionally," I thought.

"So, who are the possible suspects?" Nicole asked, climbing in beside me in the hammock—our "detective office."

"Well, there was that security guard at the museum. He looked like just the guy to do it. He was not too tall, about 5 feet 6 inches, and extremely physically fit looking. In addition, Chief Blunt said that security people are often involved, because they know the layout of the security systems and the guards' schedules."

"I don't know if she actually said 'often involved.' Besides, she could be the thief herself. She's got access to everywhere in the whole place," pointed out Nyna who had just joined us.

We paused to let that sink in for a moment.

"So maybe we'd better put both of them on our list, but I don't think the chief did it. She seemed so young and successful. Why would she want to take a risk like that? I think it's more likely to be somebody older, who's discouraged by not being successful, or making a lot of money. And, besides, any other of the security staff at the museum could have done it. But I don't think we'd be able to go meet all of them. What excuse would we have? Tell them we're famous detectives and want to interview the staff? No way!"

"And if it's one of the security staff, did he or she get hired for the job, or want to sell it on the black market?" Nyna asked.

"Yea, you're right. What if it's just some poor guy who needs money?" Nicole responded.

"The 'Trolley Man' sure could have done it. He seemed odd enough, and was really obsessed with that old history," Nicole suggested.

"But why would he want the sword? I mean, there's nothing special that we know of about the sword. If he's a collector, don't you think he'd choose something fancier or more special?" Nyna pointed out.

"He was kinda old," I pointed out, "and couldn't have done the robbery himself. But he still could have hired some guy."

"How about those fellows who want to keep the Confederate flag flying over the State House? They've sure been making a lot of noise in the news lately," suggested Nicole.

"But what reason would they have for stealing a sword? I can't even imagine why they'd steal an old Confederate flag, much less a sword. They're not trying to fly a *sword* over the capitol building, for goodness sake," Nyna said.

"Just trying to think creatively," Nicole responded. "Maybe they'd steal it to make a point of some kind. Maybe in a week or so they'll tell the television stations they've got the sword and The South Shall Rise Again."

"Oh brother. You mean like kidnapping a sword and holding it hostage? Come on!"

"What about one of the reenactors? They use and collect authentic Civil War artifacts. Maybe one of them would steal a sword, or be willing to pay for a stolen sword," Nicole suggested.

"That sure seems like too big a risk just to have an authentic weapon," Nyna remarked.

"Is there anyone else who could be a suspect?" I asked trying to move the discussion forward. I waited a moment. "So we don't know why the sword was stolen, or how, or by whom."

"Are there any clues besides the dirt?" Nyna asked.

"Well, there's the ghost, but that's not really a clue," I said, sorta joking. We didn't know what to make of the ghost. He kept showing up, and scaring the pants off us, but I couldn't figure out how he fit in. Maybe I'd check the library or the museum gift store for books about local ghosts. Could be that we'd get some help there. And maybe this ghost could give us some clues.

"I'll tell you. This whole thing's silly. We've been trying to act like big time detectives, like we're actually going to 'solve the case,'" Nicole spit out. "We're just kids with nothing else to do, and no way to get any real information or clues. I'm going to find a softball game. I'll read about whodunnit in the newspapers after the SLED agents figure it out." And Nicole left.

After she left Nyna went back in the air-conditioned house to cool off and watch soap operas.

I took up a pencil and started doodling in the scrapbook. Mrs. Baxter had found a records photo of the sword which we'd carefully pasted in. I tried to make a sketch of it. The scabbard was too intricate for me, but I drew the large eagle with outspread wings that formed the quillion which kept the hand from sliding forward onto the blade. A large eagle head right at the top, or pommel, counterbalanced the weight of the sword and was turned sideways, so that the snake he was holding in his mouth could curl down and around to join the outspread eagle wing and form a knuckle brow to protect the knuckles of the hand grasping the sword.

I turned to a clean sheet of paper and began to draw a map of the river, canal and museum. First, I drew a straight double line to represent the Gervais Street Bridge. Below the bridge the Congaree River looked like a wide tree trunk, and above the bridge the trunk separated into three strong branches, the two rivers and the canal to the right. I marked a scale of one inch = 100 feet, and placed the museum about 400 feet away from the bridge on the banks of the canal. On the bank of the Broad River, the middle branch, I marked the tunnel entrance and the old oak tree where we'd seen the ghost. I sketched the chain link fence between the museum and the canal, and the power plant, which was like a small brick dam across the canal. In pre-Civil War days, of course, the power plant wasn't there, but now the waters of the canal were channeled past huge generators and then out into the spillway through sluice gates of arched brick. I drew in the boulders in the river, the strong current of the spillway, the stone arches of the bridge, the palmetto trees planted along the street in front of the museum, and the mud landing below the bridge. Then, using a dashed line, I marked, as best I could, the path of the tunnel under the canal, to the creek opening behind the museum. "Not bad!" I thought, admiring my work.

But as I kept lying in the hammock with the bees buzzing nearby, something just started to creep up on me. The feeling was like when you fall and bang up your knee, it doesn't hurt at first but then after awhile it does start to hurt. It was as if we had forgotten something like feeding the dog, but knew there was something we'd forgotten to do. I had a little tingle thing inside me as I thought about the whole case.

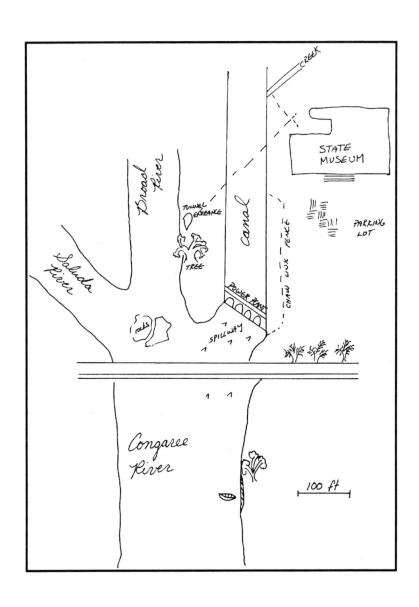

Well, we'd gotten ourselves involved, then gone to check out the scene of the crime. We talked with Mr. Jackson about the tunnels and explored the river, the State House, and the old churchyard. We talked to the chief of security at the museum, the police, and went hunting for the tunnel system. What was I missing?

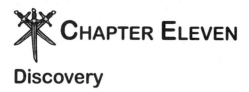

# CHAPTER ELEVEN

## Discovery

Nyna tried to revive our spirits with the ever popular choice of words, "Hey guys, let's go do something cool." Nicole thought of exploring the woods by the state park near town on this quiet, boring Sunday morning, but I took her idea and led us to the woods along the canal near the museum. She said I was obsessed with the robbery, but I was just being practical—if we were going to be exploring in the woods, why not kill two birds with one stone, and check out the woods near the museum?

This time, we started a half mile north of the museum, parked near the old Elmwood Cemetery, and clambered along the bank towards the museum. "Maybe this is where the ghost comes from!" Nicole stage whispered as we left the car. I knew she was joking because even though we'd all seen the ghost, none of us really believed in him or expected to see him again. The climb along the canal bank was miserable. There were paths that led nowhere, thorns and underbrush everywhere, slick clay from all the rain we'd been having, always the thought of snakes, particularly copperheads and water moccasins, but especially humidity so thick we could hardly breathe, and swarms of mosquitoes and no-see-ums. In our shorts and T-shirts we were a walking dinner party for these animals which buzzed in our ears and landed by our eyes.

"Whose brilliant idea was this, anyway?" Nyna complained. "I could be home, in the air conditioning, watching TV."

"Quit griping, sis. I think I see the back of the museum up there through the trees."

We left the strip of woods, and stepped carefully around the litter cluttering the edge of the old gravel lot, a great refuge for snakes and rats. A dozen or so cars were parked behind the museum. As we crossed the lot, I stopped to stare at the Confederate flags on the bumper sticker of a gray Sentra. I sensed something and looked up to see Smitty, the security guard, staring coldly at me from the window of the driver's seat, a cellular phone to his ear. Slowly, he put the phone down, opened the car door, nodded at me, and entered the employees' door of the museum.

"Come on, Rick!" Nyna shouted across the lot. I stuffed thoughts of gray Sentras and bumper stickers back into my head and joined the girls at the burnt-out storage sheds. We slowly entered a few feet into the doorway of one of the buildings. We stopped to adjust our eyes to the dimness after the glare outside. There were huge clots of dust all around us, and the brick looked kinda blackened on the inside, sorta scary.

"Is it just me, Rick, or is the hair crawling on the back of your neck, too? asked Nicole.

"No, it's just you," I replied. I didn't want to admit that the place really did give me the shivers. I thought up an evasive way to get out of the building without letting Nicole know my real reasons. "Nicole, I think we should . . ." The air suddenly chilled and darkened. In the distance I could hear deep noises, not the long rumble of thunder but thudding booms. A flicker of movement farther into the shed caught my attention.

The ghost was there, but thinner, almost transparent, just a gauze of gray uniform and pale, pale face above the thin beard of a very young man. He stared towards us, and his thin hands stretched out of the torn arms of the uniform to make scrabbling motions at a pile of dust-covered objects in the corner.

A small rat dashed across the floor, Nyna screamed, the air warmed, and the ghost disappeared. We were still frozen in the doorway, a hundred years had passed in only a moment.

We looked carefully at each other with weak grins. I wasn't scared! Were you? And together we moved carefully to the corner of the room and looked at the dust-covered pile.

"Well, here goes," I said, as I gingerly started pulling the pile apart. Dust whirled everywhere as I pulled off collapsed boxes, old newspapers, even an old canvas jacket. But there was nothing we could see that looked important. When the junk was spread all around and bare floor appeared we stopped. Then Nyna stepped forward and began rubbing her foot across the floor, spreading the dirt in trails. I leaned down to see a little hole right in the floor. If my suspicions were correct, this little hole was a trap door! I reached my hands into the hole and pulled with all my might. The floor seemed to give a little. Nicole caught on to my idea and grabbed my arms to help. We gave a final heave and fell back on our rear ends. I knew my face was red as a penny, and Nicole's face glowed with effort and there was a thick layer of sweat on her forehead. I caught my breath, and leaned forward pulling my ever present disposable flashlight from my pocket. We had pulled apart some sort of seal that lay across the trap door. We then stared down a wide, cylindrical shaft, only about six feet deep with an iron ladder fastened to the side. Below that the flashlight beam dissipated into the darkness.

"The tunnel system!" I whispered.

"Awesome, totally awesome," muttered an astonished Nicole, with Nyna leaning over her shoulder. She was the first to regain her composure. "Well, we can't just sit here in the dirt. Let us goeth toeth the adventureth, as Shakespeare would say." She grabbed the top iron rung and swung herself into the well. I had my doubts. Where did this thing lead? Would the ladder hold? Was it rusted out? Where were the rats? I was not one to be left out, but my stomach was ready for some food.

I could see Nicole crouched on the bottom rung, looking down into the dark empty space below. "Come on, Rick. It sure looks like part of that tunnel we were in. Bring the flashlight," she said. Then turning her face up she added, "What are you, chicken?"

That was the last straw, I couldn't have her use my next-to-favorite food to insult me! I jumped in after her. When I was on the rung above her, I shone the flashlight down onto a dry stone floor just another six feet below the opening to our well. Nicole supported herself on her arms, lowered herself until she was hanging, and dropped to the floor. Nyna followed me. When all three of us were clustered on the floor, I swept the flashlight beam around. The place was cool and dank, not very pleasant.

"So, how do we get back up, Sherlock?" Nyna asked.

"Don't sweat it," Nicole answered for me. "We'll either find another way out, or I'll stand on someone's shoulders, grab the ladder and get out. And then if we can't get everyone out, I can at least go get help."

"Great, Nicole," I said sarcastically, not wanting to think about waiting down there to be rescued. "Let's get on with our searching and be done with it. If we don't get out of here soon, the rumble from my stomach is going to make this place collapse!" Nicole let out a short burst of laughter, but the smile soon faded from her face and I knew there'd be no playing around in here from her. Then again, the tunnel didn't really put me in a jovial mood either. I asked the girls, then answered myself, "Which way? To the right. We should go right because the tunnel slants down in that direction, probably towards the canal, and besides, it looks lighter in that direction."

"Then maybe we should go left," Nyna said. "If we assume the tunnel goes down to the canal, we should go the other direction to see where it ends. If my sense of direction isn't turned around too much, then this other direction leads right to the museum!"

"Yeah, okay," I agreed. "But we've only got this one flashlight. So let's not go far. We've got a little light here from the opening above us. Let's not go too far away from it, so we keep oriented. We'll explore a little way to the left, then turn back and follow it down to see if it really does take us back to the canal."

We trooped up the tunnel. Forty feet or so along, it curved to the right and got darker. But it stayed level. The tunnel was tall enough for an average-sized man to walk in, but only wide enough for the three of us to walk abreast. The floor was stone blocks, and the sides were some type of metal. I kept the flashlight beam sweeping closely ahead of us, searching for loose stones, rats, and other creepy crawlies. But the tunnel was empty. After what seemed like miles, but was probably less than a city block, the tunnel ceiling lowered fairly suddenly, the floor sloped up, and we were stopped by a pile of rocks and sand.

"Should we try to push around these?" Nicole asked.

"No," Nyna responded emphatically. "We've had enough. This looks like a dead end. We're crazy to be here anyway and need to tell Dad, not just go on taking crazy chances. This place may not be safe at all, and we're stupid to explore it. We're getting out."

Nyna had suddenly remembered she was the older sister. But hearing her made me feel like an hysterical person who just got slapped back to reality. She was right. We needed to get out of there. We turned around and hurried down the now familiar tunnel and past the opening we had entered. The tunnel now slanted quickly downwards but shining the light ahead of us, we saw that it seemed to end abruptly at a stone wall.

"Oh no!" Nyna wailed.

"Wait," I said. "What's the sound?"

We all heard the sound of running water just as we reached the end of the tunnel. But it wasn't the end. It just turned so sharply to the left that we hadn't seen the opening, and it just appeared to end against the wall. We turned and the sound of the water grew louder. We walked so steeply downhill at this point that we had to bend our knees and our toes squashed into the fronts of our sneakers. But it was lightening up now, and we could see another tunnel intersecting ahead of us. We reached that point and saw water flowing from the left hand branch, dropping about four feet to our level, and then flowing off both to our right and straight ahead. Strong sunlight shone from the right-hand side.

"I know where we are!" I yelled. "Remember! This is the place we came to when we entered from the riverbank, only we were coming from the other direction! And we looked up this way and thought the tunnel ended, just like we did coming back down. I remember because after we'd slogged through all that water we could see that the tunnel rose ahead and was dry. And in the back of my mind I must have wondered why the tunnel went ahead, but then seemed to stop. So if we turn right, we'll end up in the creek!"

And sure enough, we turned right, the tunnel became wider with brick walls, granite arches, and wooden floor, and we ended at the wisteria-covered creek entrance.

\* \* \* \* \*

"So what's this contraption?" Mrs. Baxter asked my dad when she walked into the living room.

This was a special occassion. My birthday! Nicole and her mom had come over and my mom, dad, and sister were in attendance.

"It's a police scanner. I've been using it to keep up with calls during the day since I'm working night shift now."

"Hey, Dad, can't we pick up cellular phone conversations with this thing?" I asked as I reached over to adjust a few knobs. "All we ever hear on it is 'snap, crackle and pop' and some mumbled voices. You must have to take a course just to learn to understand it— 'Police Scanner Mumbo-Jumbo As a Second Language.'"

"Rick, be careful, " Dad said. "I just borrowed the scanner from the department, and if I have to return it broken, the money will come out of my paycheck and your allowance." I instantly began to handle the police scanner as if it were a priceless diamond. We listened to static, and "Roger," and mumbled incoherent relays for a few minutes. I looked around. The only one who seemed to be enjoying this was Dad. Humph! I decided that we had been through enough of this nonsense. "All right everyone, break it up. Time for presents!"

Forty-five minutes later, after we'd demolished half the cake, Mrs. Baxter and Mom left for a "constitutional" and Dad left early for his night shift at the station, and Nyna, Nicole and I hauled the scanner up on my bed. I jabbed at the power button and started adjusting the frequency. A woman's voice broke through the static. "You still have it safe?"

"Of course. You got the money?

"It's right here. You'd better bring the s—— over this evening. We close at 6:00. So come right after that."

"What was that!" I yelled. "What'd she say? Bring the s——?"

"That voice. I know it. I've heard it before!" yelled Nyna.

"Mrs. Jacobs!" Nicole and I yelled in unison, bouncing the scanner off the bed onto the floor. No matter what knobs we fiddled with after that we couldn't get that conversation back.

So, was that really Mrs. Jacobs? Was she talking about the sword? She was getting it from someone else? And paying for it. That meant the man could be the thief who actually stole the sword, and was selling it to Mrs. Jacobs. But why did she want it? And what proof did we actually have? We'd found river clay by the display case, and found some tunnels, and heard this conversation. How did they connect? Did the thief use the tunnel system? But he must have kept or hidden the sword until now. And why would Mrs. Jacobs be involved in this? She had seemed like a pretty cool lady. I reviewed our trip to the Confederate Archives. We learned a lot of history, she gave us a tour, and she even told us about her ancestor who . . . I got it! Mrs. Jacobs had an ancestor in the war—who lost his sword—whose ghost roams the riverside—in a flash the entire story was clear to me.

I leaped up. "Come on! We've got to get to the archives! I'll explain on the way!" Nyna grabbed the car keys and we flew out the back door. Our evening thunderstorm was on its way. Huge thunderheads were piling all around us and over to the west the sky was darkening. Heat lightning flickered over the trees to the north and low rumblings sounded like trucks rolling over a bridge.

The last visitor to the archives was leaving, with Mrs. Jacobs right behind to lock up when we dashed through the stinging rain to the door.

"Mrs. Jacobs! We've got to talk to you!"

"Certainly," she replied pleasantly for the benefit of the departing tourists and after a momentary pause. "Come upstairs to the office."

The storm really started pounding as we headed up the stairs. With the sudden drop in the outside temperature because of the storm, the air conditioning made the display hall almost frigid. Rain was dripping from the ornate ceiling high over our heads. Buckets and rags had already been placed in familiar places.

"This has been such a terrible summer of rain," Mrs. Jacobs said as we stopped. "Perhaps this will finally convince the state to restore this building, or at least the roof, before we have major damage. Now, what did you want to see me about."

Now that we were there, in front of her, I felt stupid. How could I imagine that this nice lady was a thief? And what could I say to her?

"Mrs. Jacobs," began Nyna, coming to my rescue. "This sounds strange. But we were listening to a police scanner, and heard a conversation about a sword, and getting money, and . . ." After a valiant try, she trailed off. But the words had their effect. Mrs. Jacobs became still, and a faint perspiration shone above her lip.

"Whatever are you talking about?"

"The Confederate sword that was stolen from the museum. Did it belong to your ancestor? Do you know anything about the theft?" Nyna was now shouting over the roar of the storm and the dripping from the ceiling.

Then we heard a new noise. A kind of crushing, tearing noise. And the drips became streams of rain pouring down around us. And we looked up as a section of the the plaster ceiling over our heads tore loose and fell down on Mrs. Jacobs, followed by great sheets of rain.

"Mrs. Jacobs, Mrs. Jacobs! Are you all right!" we screamed as we rushed to kneel beside her. She lay under a pile of rubble, eyes rolled up, but twisting her head back and forth.

"It's my sword, my grandfather's sword! I just wanted it back! Smitty said he'd get it for me and I gave him the tunnel diagrams. I promised him money, a lot of money. But it was worth it. My family sword shouldn't be on display in a museum!"

The tunnels! The thief did use the tunnels.

"Mrs. Jacobs, we're going to call for help!" I shouted at her over the noise with the rain pouring down my back. "But what about the tunnel? Where's the sword? Where did he put it?"

"The tunnel, the tunnel . . . ," she moaned, then became silent.

# CHAPTER TWELVE

## The Chase

---

Thinking quickly I said, "Where is a phone? I need to call 911 for an ambulance."

"How about calling Dad?" Nyna said.

"We'd better get help for Mrs. Jacobs first. Dad would just call for an ambulance himself."

I looked at the floor where Mrs. Jacobs lay, trapped beneath a pile of rotten ceiling, with the cold rain pouring down on her. There was dirt, plaster, water, and a little blood all around the floor. I hoped she would be all right.

"Quick, Rick, help me drag this table over. We can slide it over Mrs. Jacobs and at least keep some of the rain off her," Nyna yelled over the sound of the rain pouring through the ceiling. "And we'd better not even try to get that rubble off her. We might make the situation worse!" We grabbed a large formica-topped table and hauled it toward her. We half dragged and half carried it over chunks of ceiling tiles and soggy insulation. Somewhere in the back of my mind sounded the clicking and whirring of warnings about electrical wiring and water, but in the dust and rain and confusion I could see almost nothing.

Nicole pulled me to a phone in the museum office and I grabbed the receiver off the hook. Should I call

Dad's beeper number? No, we weren't going to wait for him to call back. Should I just tell the 911 dispatcher what we were going to do? No, I needed to tell Dad. I dialed the information number for the police department. With any luck, an officer I knew would answer the phone. Yes, thank goodness! "Officer Blevins, this is Rick Black. Tell my dad that we're at the Confederate Museum. The roof collapsed on Mrs. Jacobs and we need an ambulance. We think the sword thief is somewhere over by the State Museum right now, so we're heading over there—COME FIND US!"

Long minutes later the ambulance sirens blared loudly outside the museum, and we ran down to the lobby. "Where do you need help?" one of the arriving medics asked.

"Upstairs. The roof collapsed on the director of the museum!" Then I turned to the girls and said, "Come on, let's get the thief."

We ran, heads down and rain running down the backs of necks, got into the car, slammed the doors, and pulled out into the street. The sky was dark like night, the wind was fierce with lightning flashing and thunder booming in the light. The storm must have been right on top of us. Nyna had the windshield wipers on full speed and the foot long metal sticks seemed to be in as much a hurry as we were. We were only a mile away from the museum but the drive seemed to take hours. The wipers whipped back and forth, back and forth, trying to clear the windshield of the rain. From the front seat Nyna and I leaned against the dashboard trying to see the road past the front of the car.

"Slow down!" I yelled. "You can't see a thing out there!"

"Speed up!" yelled Nicole from the back seat. "You're doing fine! We gotta catch that thief!"

When we finally got to the museum it had seemed like I could have walked there faster. But there was no time for thinking—we drove straight to the outbuild-ings and parked regardless of parking spaces or other cars. Besides, there was still so much rain and so little light, that no one was anywhere near. I was glad that we always kept flashlights in the car.

"Come on, let's go."

We bailed out of the car and dashed under cover, shook off for a moment, and caught our breath.

"Now what?" I asked. "Are we nuts? Where are we going to look for him?"

"Maybe he's armed!" Nicole moaned.

"With what? A dull, hundred-year-old sword?" Nyna said scornfully.

"This place gives me the creeps. I'm not going back in that tunnel," I said.

"We've got to. Come on, Rick, we haven't got any time to lose," said Nyna heading back into the corner where the well-like tunnel opening was still exposed. Nobody had been back in the old storage area since us. We stuck the flashlights in our pockets, slipped down the well ladder, and dropped to the tunnel floor. For a few minutes we shuffled and stamped our feet, trying to get our bearings and eyesight back in the feeble light that shafted through the opening. The stone floor was dry, but the tunnel was dark and creepy as it stretched away from our spot. The sound of the rain was still so loud that it masked all the noise we made so we saw the thief a lot sooner than we ex-pected. As we huddled in the darkness before decid-ing whether to head down to the river or up towards the museum, a figure cloaked entirely in black hurtled down the tunnel into us! He stopped abruptly and we stared shocked and openmouthed at each other.

For a split second I thought, "Geez, is this real?"

"It's Smitty!" Nicole yelled with no hesitation. Time froze for a moment. What to do? I felt like I was watching the entire scene on TV, with me, and the girls, paralyzed against the tunnel wall, and Smitty towering over us like a giant bat. Would he chase us? Hurt us? Could we talk to him? Say, "Hey Smitty, how's the museum?" Could we just stop this crazy scene and go home?

"After him!" Nicole yelled again. Now I had proof that she watched too much TV. The moment unfroze as Smitty turned swiftly and ran back up the tunnel. Nicole dashed after him, Nyna followed immediately, and I slowly pumped my legs after them both, feeling as if I were running in mud, or running in a dream. As I ran my brain was working about as hard as my legs. A billion thoughts were moving around. How long could the tunnel be? Unless it continued under the river it couldn't be more than a few hundred feet. Smitty took a sharp turn. Like magic I knew where we were going; the thief was going back to the museum to try to lose us!

"This is the way to the museum!" I yelled to Nicole.

Smitty seemed to know his way in the dark, but I yanked my flashlight out and the beam waved crazily across the floor creating weird shadows across the stones. The walls closed heavily in around me. My panting breath sounded like a freight train in my head, and the thudding of our feet echoed from the walls.

As we neared the end of the tunnel the floor leveled out. I estimated about a quarter mile to the museum, actually, it was probably only a few hundred feet. Suddenly the thief took a little hop and bounced out of sight. Nicole, close behind him, and not thinking, did the same thing. She scrambled past rocks and sand and crashed through a trapdoor, with Nyna and me following. I heard a few muffled sounds, I think they were:

"Ouch!"

And . . .

"Watch your head!"

We found ourselves in a narrow, shoulder-width space, between two gray walls. We were abruptly out of the underground tunnel and into the building. Sudden light filtered in, disorienting us again. The thief, ahead of us, had pushed one of the walls aside—the three of us followed.

"We're in the Gift Shop!" Nyna exclaimed.

Smitty sprinted to the doors, tipping over display tables of books and stuffed animals behind him.

"Watch out!" Nicole yelled, as she scrambled over a pile of expensive debris. Nyna hurdled a small table, and I tripped over it, sprawling into a case of fancy cheese grits, pralines, and chocolate-covered pecans. Nicole kept running and Nyna only slowed a moment, looking back at me, before racing on.

The alarms began sounding loudly, set off as Smitty ran out of the shop, with the girls on his tail, and me stumbling after them across the lobby. Now out the main door, and out of the tunnel, on familiar ground where we could all see, Smitty really began to run. The sky was heavy and gray, and the air thick, but I finally caught my breath and the adrenaline started to flow now that I was outside and away from the claustrophobic unreal nightmare of the tunnel.

Down the drive we raced, legs flying, with Smitty a solid black shape ahead of us. We were a ragged line of runners as we crossed the parking lot, dodged the few cars still parked about, splashed through puddles, and headed down the embankment to the chain link fence by the canal.

I raced past Nyna and joined up with Nicole as we slowed along the slick, muddy path. We grabbed hold of the fence, clawing at the links as we squinted through the rain.

"He's getting ahead of us!" Nicole yelled to me as we sped up again and ran around the edge of the fence towards the power plant stretched across the water where it flowed rapidly through arched sluice gates to join the river below. Smitty effortlessly scaled the chain link fence and disappeared down the bank.

"Geez, he's heading into the power plant!" I yelled as Nicole and I awkwardly started pulling ourselves up and over the fence. We shuffled down the bank, trying to run without losing balance, but actually half slid and half rolled down to the large open doors at one end of the power plant. We ran in. Three huge generators marched ahead of us, rising from the violent waters below. We found ourselves running along a narrow, iron-fenced walkway which encircled the generators high above the river.

"Where is he? Can you see him?" Nicole panted. I just pointed, too scared by the unsteady feeling of the rushing and roaring river below me, to do anything but concentrate on straight ahead and the doors leading back onto firm ground. We ran into the rain and on to blessed ground again. The bank was covered with sharp clumps of grass and gouged-out clay channels filled with rivulets of water flowing down the hill. We scrambled and slipped up across the small end of land which was a peninsula protruding like a gnarled old finger between the end of the canal and the river. I couldn't see Smitty anymore, and was so tired and blinded by the rain that I hardly knew what I was doing or why I was doing it. But Nicole sprinted ahead of me and across the riverbank. I gave my last effort to run and went almost out of control as the bank tipped sharply downward by the river's edge near the tunnel entrance. I slid to a stop next to Nicole in the mud and rain by the large oak tree.

"Where is he?" I whispered loudly against the noise of the rain.

"Shh! Look!"

Just ahead, crouched by the tunnel entrance was a dark figure. Then I saw the sword in his hand, the brass dragon head and engraved scabbard gleaming in the shaft of pink and orange light that was just breaking through the western clouds. Nicole crouched into a runner's start, then in an instant dashed forward and leaped onto the thief's back, wrestling him to the ground. I caught up, and sliding in the mud like someone stealing home plate, cut his legs out from under him. But as I did that I was lost among a jumble of shouts, some of them my own.

"Get him down, Rick!"

"Jump on his back, Nicole!"

"I did!"

"Where's Nyna?"

"Grab the sword!"

Then heaving Nicole off his back, Smitty stood, arms wide above his head. Swinging the sword around his head as we fell back, he yelled and flung the sword as far as he could into the swirling waters of the river rapids.

As he turned back towards us, Nicole took a small hop and step, and with a snapping scissors kick, cracked his jaw. As he crumpled to the ground we turned to the river.

The pink and orange light had become the glow of the bridge burning behind us. Smoke filled the air, cannons boomed in the distance and drums sounded across the river. The sword, still gleaming, floated towards the burning bridge, caught in debris of branches and leaves. A small splash, and the young ghost of the Confederate soldier rose from the water near the pile of debris and took the sword in his hand, lifted it above his head and looked straight across the dark water at us. A final clap of thunder rolled above us and in that instant a bolt of lightning slit through the air and struck the old gnarled oak tree near me on the water's edge with a blast like the sound of a bomb exploding. Struck motionless by the sound and light, I saw, as in slow motion, the tree split completely in half. Inside the tree, glowing with reflected light, were a skull and and a pile of bones. As my eyes readjusted, and my limbs started to shake, the bones fell, tumbling softly over each other to the ground.

# CHAPTER THIRTEEN

## The Bones of Jonathan Jacobs

---

Sirens wailed on the bridge. Nyna, standing on the bridge, and terrified we'd been hurt by the lightning, hailed the police cars desperately.

Dad arrived with other police officers. They ran across the spillway, scrambled down to us, handcuffed the thief and congratulated us on our good work, commenting about the "Hardy Boys coming true," along with the customary, that-was-very-dangerous-you-could-have-been-hurt lecture. Dad was disappointed to learn that the sword had been lost, though we just told him the thief had thrown it in the river, not about the ghost.

"We'll search the river then. SLED agents are on their way—this is their case, really. But let's see who this fellow is." Dad walked over to the thief, who'd been handcuffed and read his Miranda Rights by one of the other police officers. "Do you know who this is?"

\* \* \* \* \*

The rain had stopped, and the evening sky was lighter. Mist hung above the street as we three sat in Dad's patrol car, waiting for him to finish with the SLED agents. We'd stood out in the drizzle, shivering with wet exhaustion, while we told the SLED agents our story, giving them enough evidence to arrest the thief. Now I could do nothing but think, aghast, about the sword, the lightning, and the bones, until Nyna spoke. "Mrs. Jacobs's great-grandfather, the young Confederate soldier who died and disappeared when Sherman marched on Columbia and the city burned—maybe he hid in that tree when he was wounded so that the enemy couldn't get him. And that's what we saw happen that day we canoed up the river."

I nodded my head, "Maybe."

"And those are his bones down there."

"And when he rubbed his hand up and down his leg and looked at us, he was trying to tell us to find his missing sword," Nicole added.

"So the ghost got the sword, after a century and a half."

"Well, I hope he is happy and at peace now," said Nicole.

"Yes," I said. "He is happy and free of walking the riverside. He's got his sword back, and I guess his bones will be buried properly. Now he can do whatever it is that ghosts do when they've finished their business here."

# CHAPTER FOURTEEN

## Aftermath

"Mrs. Diana Jacobs, the Director of the Confederate Archives, died toda  from heart failure," the car radio announced as Nicole reached over to turn up the volume. "She had br en hospitalized following the collapse of the Archives' roof during a violent thunderstorm last week. Mrs. Jacobs confessed to police that she hired Mr. Turner Smith, a security guard at the State Museum, to steal a Confederate sword which she claimed belonged to her great-grandfather and was rightfully hers. More on that story, and on the latest developments in the Confederate flag controversy, after . . ."

"I never thought she'd actually die," said Nicole a bit sadly. "But she wasn't young, and she was sure in a lot of trouble. I think I'd rather die than have to go to jail."

"Some summer this has been," I sighed. We were returning home from the old Confederate Cemetery which lay on the banks of the river upstream from the museum, and which had been the location of the Yankee attack on Columbia back in 1865. A small crowd, including museum officials, historians, police, and TV cameras and reporters had just laid Jonathan Jacobs's bones to rest in a shady spot under the oak trees.

Over the grave was placed a small stone marker, scribed "C.S.A.," for the Confederate States of America. Finally, after 130 years, the bones of the Confederate ghost were buried with his fellow soldiers.

"WBRC News," a voice invaded the interior of the car. "Here we are outside the State House where the flag controversy continues. When will the controversy stop? Will the courts decide? Will the legislators assume the responsibility to resolve this dilemma?"

"Oh, those crazy fools, again," jested Nicole. "Turn the radio down!"

"Dad told us the thief got into the museum by crawling through those big ventilation pipes that are suspended from the ceiling. He dropped out right by the display case, so was able to avoid the alarms until he broke the glass! I think the SLED agents already knew how he got in and out, just didn't know who he was!"

"Did y'all see the newspaper today?" asked Nicole, turning the corner towards home.

"No, why?" Nyna asked.

"Well, right next to the photograph of Mrs. Baxter, textile restoration expert, and her heroic daughter, was a report that the Historic Preservation Society is looking into excavating and restoring the tunnels. Smitty turned over Mrs. Jacobs's diagrams to SLED, and they'll be released to the Preservation Society once the trial's over. If the tunnels only lead to the museum, they may become part of the museum exhibits, but if they actually do go all the way downtown, then the city will treat them like an historic site. But right now it seems most likely that they were built as overflow drains to protect the canal, not as a transportation system."

"Speaking of heroes," Nyna added, "I think the police department isn't sure whether to give a commendation directly to us, or to Dad for having such heroic kids!"

jlad it's all over," I said. "Being a
ıll it's cracked up to be. I think I want
st of the summer in the hammock, or
ɔl."

u forgetting something?" Nyna asked as
we ▁ ▁ ɔ our driveway.

"What?"

"Remember, you have three newpaper articles to write, and your deadline is the day after tomorrow!"

"My articles!"